Praise for *Catching Jordan*

"I stayed up all night reading *Catching Jordan*—I couldn't put it down! Jordan Woods is my heroine!"

—Simone Elkeles, *New York Times* bestselling author of the *Perfect Chemistry* series

"Sweetly satisfying."

—*VOYA*

"*Catching Jordan* has it all: heart, humor, and a serious set of balls. With a clever, authentic voice, Kenneally proves once and for all that when it comes to making life's toughest calls—on and off the field—girls rule!"

—Sarah Ockler, bestselling author of *Fixing Delilah* and *Twenty Boy Summer*

"Jordan is a compelling protagonist, an appealing mix of confidence and vulnerability…This is a solid, substantive romance that makes all the right moves for girls who won't settle for a seat on the sidelines, in love or on the field."

—*Bulletin of the Center for Children's Books*

"I fell in love with the hero on page 1, and *Catching Jordan* just gets better from there. This feel-good romantic comedy about high school football is the novel I've been waiting for. I loved it!"

—Jennifer Echols, author of *Such a Rush*

"Kenneally makes football accessible—and even enjoyable—for those who might not ordinarily follow the sport...Jordan (or "Woods," as her teammates call her) is a fearless captain and the teamwork and camaraderie that's so implicit in the story are great takeaways for readers of any age."

—*RT Book Review*, 4 stars

"A beautiful novel with a competitive spirit both on and off the field. With a real and captivating depiction of high school relationships, *Catching Jordan* shows the same reverence for the human heart that it does for the game of football."

—Karsten Knight, author of *Wildefire*

Stealing Parker

Stealing Parker

MIRANDA KENNEALLY

sourcebooks
fire

Published by Sourcebooks Fire, an imprint of Sourcebooks, Inc.
P.O. Box 4410, Naperville, Illinois 60567-4410
(630) 961-3900
Fax: (630) 961-2168
teenfire.sourcebooks.com

Library of Congress Cataloging-in-Publication data is on file with the publisher.

Printed and bound in the United States of America.
VP 10 9 8 7 6 5 4 3 2 1

for all the girls struggling to find their place

the day i met brian hoffman

52 days until i turn 18

Bubblegum Pink is the nail polish of the day.

Matt Higgins will definitely like it—he's into all things girly-girl, so I add another coat before blowing on my nails. Tonight we're meeting at this field party, and I fully expect we'll make out behind a hay bale or something.

Drew is lounging on my bed, reading *Cosmo*. "So I signed you up to be manager for my baseball team."

"What?!" Careful not to mess up my polish, I mute the TV and sit up to face him. "Why?"

"I can't stand the idea of you holed up in your room while I'm playing ball this spring. You should come to practice tomorrow morning." He smells a perfume ad, cringes and sticks his tongue out.

My heart pounds faster than light speed. I hate baseball. I know, I know. That means I'm not a true American. It probably means I'm not human. But I gave up foam fingers, peanuts, and the Atlanta Braves when my mom announced she's a lesbian and ran off with her friend who was more than just a friend. A year ago January, she divorced my dad, and I divorced her dreams of me playing softball for Hundred Oaks.

"No way," I say, examining my nails.

"Come on, Parker!" He thumbs through the magazine. "Please?" he whines.

"What's involved?" I try to act nonchalant, but Drew looks up with a knowing smile. He's lived down the street from me my whole life—I'll do anything for him.

"Taking stats and helping with equipment."

Taking stats is way easy. I could do it in my sleep.

"It'll be a cinch," Drew says, reading my mind. He shows me a cartoon couple using a dining room table for Kama Sutra maximum effect. "Jesus Christ," he says. "Is that move physically possible?"

"Try it out with Amy and let me know."

He glances at me sideways, then turns the magazine vertical and studies it closely. "I'm flexible, but not that flexible."

"Can you imagine needing a hip replacement at seventeen? You could get a cane with flames painted on it."

"Or maybe one with skulls."

"Pirate ships!"

"Don't change the subject…So there'll be plenty of guys for you on the team." He snorggles. That's our special word for snorting and giggling. It'll be in *Webster's* any day now.

I have to admit I love the way cute guys look in baseball uniforms. Plus, I'd get to spend more time with Drew. Lately, his idea of fun has been going to Jiffy Burger with Corndog and Sam Henry and acting like they're the characters from *Seinfeld*, talking about nothing. Drew invites me along sometimes when they need an Elaine, because I'm really good at punching Corndog (George Costanza) and yelling "Get out!" and Drew says I dance worse than the real Elaine. But it's been getting kinda old. How many times can those guys debate who has better fries: Sonic or Jiffy Burger?

And what else do I have to do this semester? It's February, I've got a 4.0, and classes don't matter at this point—the only way Vanderbilt could revoke my early admission would be if I went on the news and advocated for Tennessee to secede from the union.

On the other hand, this could be a lot of work. I'd probably end up doing hard stuff like lugging water coolers around and washing dirty jockstraps or something.

On the other hand, I don't want to be lonely.

Jockstraps it is.

• • •

When I was five, Mom discovered a recipe for homemade edible Play-Doh. We loved cooking together, especially fancy stuff like foie gras grilled cheese. We sat at the kitchen table, which was covered by the previous week's comics, and mixed flour and sugar and peanut butter together and rolled it into shapes. I had dinosaur cookie cutters, so I made a Play-Doh T-Rex. Mom made a triceratops. I bit its head off, and she joked, "My little praying mantis." We giggled and giggled and gorged ourselves on that Play-Doh. The next day we went to church and Mom and I kneeled at the altar. As I prayed, I didn't ask you for anything. I only thanked you for giving me Mom.

Written on February 12 before the party at Morton's field. Burned using a candle.

• • •

On Saturday morning, Drew and I arrive at the baseball field behind Hundred Oaks High—aka the only place I dread more than Chuck E. Cheese (I worked there last summer and almost died because I had to wear a Crusty the Cat costume).

We step out of his red VW bug into the sun, and the crisp wind bites my face. I pull my arms up inside my fleece and begin the trek across the parking lot to meet the players, who are warming up by doing throwing exercises and sprints. I stare at the most popular guys at our school.

Popular-schmopular—any cute guy will do. Last Sunday after church? I hung out with this guy Aaron on the swings at the playground, listening to him talk about how much his school sucks (he goes to Woodbury High) and how Nirvana really is the best band ever. I disagree—I'm into modern stuff like Paramore and the All-American Rejects, but I couldn't get a word in because he kept talking and talking and talking. Before he drove home with his parents, I let him kiss me beside the turtle sandbox thing, so people will know I like boys.

"Over here!" Coach Burns calls, beckoning us.

"Oh, dear me," I croon to Drew. "Your coach is older than baseball itself."

"I think he coached my grandpa."

"And his grandpa."

"Everyone's been saying he'll retire after this year. Would you rather retire or work your whole life?"

"I'd retire tomorrow if I could, and I haven't even started working yet," I reply. "When you retire, would you rather spend time playing golf or bingo?"

"Golf. I love the outfits. Golf or polo?" he asks.

"Do you mean water polo or horse polo?"

"Water."

"Gross. I like animals much more than speedos."

Drew introduces me to the coach, who starts explaining my responsibilities. How I'll be the official statistician because I make straight As in calc. (Coach did his homework.) How I should always have the coolers filled with ice water before practices start, and how I should make sure the buckets by the pitching machines are loaded with balls. Drew snorggles at the mention of balls. Perv. I elbow him.

"You should always be thirty minutes early for practice." The coach clears his throat, and his lined face goes a bit pink. He glances at Drew, then back to me. "And if you decide to date or mess around with anyone on the team, you can't be a manager anymore, okay?"

What? Kissing players is reason numero uno I'm willing to sit around watching these guys belch and adjust their crotches and spit in the dugout.

"Why?" I ask, scrunching my eyebrows.

"The girl who managed the team last year, uh, well, we had some incidents on the bus and in the locker room." He coughs. "I'm sure that won't happen with you."

Does he think I'm incapable of getting guys? I kissed Matt Higgins behind a barn last night. Trust me, I'm capable of getting a guy.

I smooth my curve-enhancing blue fleece. I'm wearing leather boots over skinny jeans. It's not sporty attire, but I once read this book called *The Rules* that said guys like girls who always look ready to go on a date, so I even wear lip gloss when jogging. The only thing I never bother fixing is my tangled waist-length brown hair. It may sound gross, but my hair looks good tangly—guys love it.

"No worries, Coach," I say.

Coach tells Drew to warm up, so he runs off, his cleats clacking on the asphalt. "You should meet my new assistant coach and our new captain. Don't take orders from any guys except the captain, understand?"

I nod, and Coach Burns calls out, "Hoffman! Whitfield! Get over here!"

Corndog, aka Will Whitfield, swings at a pitch, drops his bat, then jogs over. He must truly love baseball to smile in 40-degree February weather. He tosses away his batting helmet and runs his fingers through the brown waves of his hair before pulling his cap from the back pocket of his baseball pants.

"Hey," he says, giving me a bright grin, showing off the dimple in his right cheek.

Yeah, yeah. I know you're hot, Corndog. I fight the urge to roll my eyes. Thanks to all the years he's spent baling hay on his dad's farm, Corndog has gone from not to hot, from scrawny to sinewy, from geek to god, and now has to beat girls off with a stick. Not that he ever dates. Not that I'd ever hook up with him. He nearly became valedictorian instead of me.

"So…" he whispers, putting his hat on. "You and Higgins, eh?"

I pull my knit cap down over my ears and tell myself to ignore the queasiness. I didn't enjoy kissing Matt Higgins very much. He kept trying to go up my shirt. "It was a one-night thing."

Corndog removes a batting glove. "Isn't it always, for you?" He laughs, but it's not a nice laugh, and gives me a hard stare. "You keep screwing with my friends."

I rub my neck. What he's saying isn't a lie. I do kiss guys a lot.

And I'd be lying if I said I'm not interested in snuggling or talking on the phone late at night, falling asleep talking to a boy I'm in love with. I do want a boyfriend. But I haven't met any guys worth the risk of being ditched.

"Just do me a favor," Corndog whispers. "Don't mess with Bates."

I raise my eyebrows. I've never had that kind of spark with Drew. We had our diapers changed together. Besides, he's been dating this sweet girl, Amy Countryman, for like half his life. She enjoys knitting and cooks him breakfast for dinner. But truth be told, I'm not entirely sure Drew likes only girls.

"You don't have to worry about Drew," I whisper.

"Thanks." Corndog nods.

"Would you two like to join us sometime today?" Coach Burns says, motioning toward the field. "I want Parker to meet the new coach."

That's when a baseball rolls up to my boots.

"Sorry! Foul ball," Sam calls from home plate, clutching his bat.

I scoop up the ball, wind my arm, and hurl it from the parking lot and over the fence to shortstop.

"Wow," a voice says. "She's got a hell of an arm."

I turn slowly, and that's when I first see him.

His tan face is thin with stubble and a strong jaw. He's a couple inches taller than my 5'7". He's wearing gray baseball pants, an oversized black sweatshirt cut off at the elbows, and a frayed beige ball cap. Dark curls sneak out from under the brim. His big brown eyes meet mine and my breath sputters.

"Hi," Beautiful Boy says, stretching out a hand. "I'm Brian Hoffman, the new assistant coach."

"Parker Shelton."

Somehow I shake his hand and squeak out my name. Names, names. Brian & Parker sounds like a law firm. Parker & Brian sounds like a pharmaceutical company. His calloused palm feels rough against mine. I picture him touching my hair.

"Do you play softball?" Coach Hoffman asks me, smiling. He raises an eyebrow.

"No."

"You should try out."

I'm still shaking his hand. Longest Handshake of All Time.

Maybe we can shake hands until practice is over and then I'll ask if he wants to hang out.

Wait. This guy's a coach. How old is he? Twenty-one? Twenty-two?

I release his hand and wipe my tingling palm on my jeans. Corndog's shaking his head at me. Coach Hoffman beckons for us to follow him onto the field. My pulse races as I cross the fresh chalk of the first base line. This is the first time I've stepped foot on a diamond in a year.

We meet the team at home plate, where Coach Hoffman tells them I'm the new manager. The guys crowd around me, saying stupid things like "Parker Shelton, woooo!" and "I love you, Parker!" and "Parker Shelton, I want to have all your babies!" and I shove my hands in the pockets of my fleece, glancing between the guys and the ground. Normally I'd be grinning, but I don't want Bri—I mean, Coach Hoffman seeing me act desperate.

Coach Burns takes this moment to tell the guys to keep their hands off me or risk getting suspended for two games. Then he leads the pitchers to the outfield for long toss.

"Coach Burns must really be pissed about last year," Paul Briggs says under his breath to Sam, but loud enough for me to hear. Paul plays catcher, and his weight rivals that of an orca whale. He gestures at me. "Sucks we won't be getting hot managerial play. Everyone knows she puts out."

"Shut up, man," Sam says, slapping Paul with a glove.

Corndog glares at Paul. "Apologize now."

Paul shrugs. "Sorry."

"Don't be an ass," Coach Hoffman tells Paul, grabbing him by a sleeve. "Five laps."

Paul throws him a look of hatred but takes off ambling around the field. Paul's not even capable of jogging.

I toe the ground, wishing someone would squash me into the red clay.

Coach Hoffman steps closer, his face turning rosy. Freckles dot his nose. His lips are chapped. Does he bite them?

He whispers, "I'm sorry about that."

"No big deal," I say, folding my arms across my chest. I want to tell him that I don't technically put out. I'm still a virgin. Honestly, I still have problems using tampons. They just don't work for me. I even studied this diagram in *Seventeen* that gave tips on how to get them in, but I can't figure out the logistics. And sometimes trying to figure it out makes blood rush to my head and I feel like I might pass out and I can only imagine Dad finding me in the bathroom, unconscious next to the toilet, pants-less with a tampon in my hand.

As if I'd ever ask my mother for tampon tips.

Coach Hoffman directs the JV guys to the batting cages and sends the varsity onto the field, to scrimmage. He adjusts his beige cap, looking at me. "Let's go over how to take stats, okay?"

"Okay, sounds great." Not that I need help with stats. I'm so good, I bet the Braves would hire me. But he doesn't have to know that.

Coach Hoffman goes on, "I'll need you to take stats at practices too. I'm in charge of the lineup, so accurate stats are crucial to my decision-making process."

His decision-making process? Crazy mature.

"Okay, Coach."

"Coach?" He lets out a ripple of laughter. "I don't think I'll ever get used to kids calling me coach or mister."

He thinks of us as kids? "How old are you, if you don't mind me asking?" My voice shakes.

He pauses. "I'm twenty-three. Just finished up my master's in phys ed at Georgia Tech."

He's a complete adult. He's six—one, two, three, four, five, six—years older than me. "What class are you teaching?"

"Gym, but I'm not sure what my schedule is yet." He pulls his cap off and puts it back on. He chomps on his gum. "They hired me to take over the baseball team for Coach Burns when he retires next year."

"So it's true?"

Coach Hoffman nods. "I'm in training this season."

As far as coaching goes, working at Hundred Oaks in Franklin is an impressive job to have. Our Raiders usually make it to the district tournament, if not further.

"You must know your baseball," I say.

He gives me a long serious look. I see his Adam's apple shift as he swallows. "Something like that."

"Did you play?" I ask.

"Something like that." His face goes hard.

"They must call you Cryptic Coach Hoffman." We haven't taken one step away from home plate.

"I'm never gonna get used to being called coach. Seriously."

I laugh lightly. "How about a nickname?"

"Such as?" He raises his eyebrows.

I stuff my frozen hands in my armpits. "The Hoff?"

"Isn't that David Hasselhoff's nickname?"

"Perhaps."

"So you're equating me with that movie star guy who gets trashed and videotapes himself drunk and eating cheeseburgers?"

"Exactly."

"Back in high school they called me Shooter."

"Why? Are you a deer hunter or something?"

"Uhhh, you don't want to know what it means." The side of his mouth quirks up.

I rock back and forth on my heels. "I like the Hoff way better."

He smiles at me. "If you're gonna call me the Hoff, I'm gonna give you a nickname too."

"Such as…?"

"Trouble. I'll call you Trouble."

"Cliché."

"Touché."

We start laughing.

"God, this is the silliest conversation I've had in ages," he says with a smile.

Yeah, probably because you're an adult and I'm a child, and how could an adult possibly have a normal mature conversation with a girl? I gaze down at the red clay beneath my boots, then look up into his brown eyes and sneak a glimpse at the loose curls peeking out from under his hat. Are they soft?

I say, "Fine, you can call me Trouble. And I'm still gonna call you the Hoff."

His face contorts into this blend of pain and amusement. "Call me Brian," he says quietly. "I'm not ready to be called coach or mister. I'm not ancient."

"Brian." I like the way it sounds coming off my tongue. Full and deep. His mouth slides into a smile, and I catch him quickly scanning my body.

He leads me over to the dugout, picking up a stick along the way. We sit down. He hands me a pencil and the stats book, which looks like a large, floppy sketchpad. Boxes of tiny field grids fill the inside pages. I bring the stats book to my nose and inhale the smoky gray paper.

Brian laughs softly and uses the stick to clean clay out of his cleats. "You must really like baseball. Smelling the stats book and all."

"Smelling books is a habit Dad got me started on."

"There are worse habits." Brian shows me his fingernails. He's bitten them down to the quick. How personal. It's not like I openly show people my super-long second toes.

"You ever taken stats before?" he asks. I like his voice. Low, Southern, manly.

"Sort of," I say, tracing my palm. "Dad is a big Braves fan." *Was* a big Braves fan.

"Me too." He goes back to picking wet clay and grass out of his cleat. "What's your team?"

"Braves, I guess." I want to keep talking to him. I can do this. I can talk about baseball again. When my family was still together, we loved heading down to Atlanta on weekends to catch games, especially when they played the Phillies and the Mets.

Mom played softball in high school, and then went on to play shortstop for the University of Tennessee. Before she ditched us, I played softball too. I loved it. But last January, when she left and moved to Knoxville with Theresa, our family was embarrassed to the nth degree. Everyone at church gave us funny looks on Sundays during Coffee Time in the Fellowship Hall, which is a fancy way of saying we eat stale donuts in the church basement. I don't even know why we kept going to church.

"But why would we want to hang out with those jerks who judge us because of something Mom did?" I had cried to Dad.

"It's just a phase. They'll forget about it."

"But—"

"We are not negotiating this," he replied, studying the newspaper.

"Are we going to atone for Mom's sins?" my older brother asked.

"Becoming a lesbian is a sin?" I replied.

"I'm not sure. People at church think so." Ryan sucked on his bottom lip.

"Does it actually say that in the Bible? Thou shalt not become a lesbian?"

"No," Dad said with a sigh, his eyes closed.

"Then why are we going to church?" I blurted. Phase or not, how the congregation turned on us didn't seem forgivable.

"We trust in prayer," Dad replied. His father believes in prayer. So did his grandfather.

Church means dressing up on Sunday mornings and forgoing French toast at the kitchen table for stale powdered donuts. It means listening to Brother John saying "Your body is a temple" and "True love waits," and then we all would say we'll wait until we get married to have sex. Or at least until college.

Some people at church thought I might turn out like my mom. A lesbian. A sinner. I overheard the youth pastor whispering that to the choir director. Brother John told Mrs. James that they would always love me, but he and his wife had to protect their daughter, Laura (my former best friend), from making similarly bad choices. I went home and hid all my pictures of Mom and cried and cried.

But that made me feel worse, because I knew Mom adored me, and no matter how hard she had tried to hide it, we could tell she was depressed. Before she left Dad, sometimes I came home from school and found she'd been crying.

I used to love church, but I turned away from it like they turned on me. I shouldn't have been surprised. After Tate Gillam's dad got caught doing his secretary, my own dad told me not to hang around Tate and his sister Rachel anymore.

When I confronted Laura about what her dad had said, that I might turn out like my mom—a lesbian, a sinner—we got into a huge fight because I said her father wasn't being a good Christian toward me. Laura asked, "What do you know about being a Christian? You knew I liked Jack Hulsey. When you turned him down to the Winter Wonderland formal, you could've put in a good word for me. But you only care about yourself and proving you're better than me."

So untrue.

Our frustrations had been building up for a long time anyhow, so she didn't take it well when I called her a jealous bitch. The words popped out and I wanted to take them back, but I couldn't.

Then Laura spread a rumor around school, saying I'm just like my mom. *A butch softball player who probably likes girls.*

Apparently "love thy neighbor" changes to "judge thy neighbor" if your family doesn't follow the church playbook.

Where did you go, God?

That night after Laura spread the rumors, I started dieting. I went from 140 pounds of muscle down to 110 pounds of skin and bone and hotness. I look good. I don't look butch. All the guys know I look good. They know I want them and that I love kissing and sometimes rounding a couple bases (I never go further than second). But that's as close as they're getting. Emotionally or otherwise.

"Hello? Earth to Parker." Brian snaps his fingers in my face.

"Oh. Sorry."

"What're you thinking about?"

I hear a crack: the ball connecting with a bat. Foul ball. Drew

14

stands at second base, pounding a fist into his glove. Corndog mans third, hunched over on his knees, focused on the batter. Brian smacks bubblegum that smells like heaven.

After Mom left, we stopped watching the Braves.

"I'm thinking about baseball," I whisper.

"Oh yeah?" A grin sneaks on his face. "I love this game."

• • •

Lee Miller pops up to center field. Sam catches the fly, then lobs the ball to shortstop.

Brian asks, "Why'd you want to be our manager?"

"Drew wanted me to." I gesture toward second base, where I can see him standing on tiptoes, trying to see what I'm up to. "He's my best friend."

"That's cool," he says. "Are you a senior?"

"Yep."

"Where do you want to go to college?"

"Vanderbilt?" I don't tell him I've already been accepted early decision.

He whistles. "Good school."

"My brother Ryan goes there. He still lives at home with us, though." Vanderbilt's only about 20 minutes away.

"You're close with your family?" Brian asks.

"Sorta close with my dad and Ryan." I peek over at him. "How about you? Do you have any brothers or sisters?"

Brian watches a cloud passing overhead. "A little sister. Anna…What about your mom?"

I blush. "Um, she doesn't live here anymore."

He finds my eyes, but doesn't press further. "Anna doesn't live here anymore either. She moved to Florida."

"Do you miss her?" *Because I miss Mom and the way things were before the divorce so much…all I want is for everyone in my family to be whole again. For us to be whole together.*

Brian chews his gum. "It's a scary thing to wake up and realize the people you need most aren't nearby anymore…But you keep moving."

He elbows me, and yeah, he's much older, but I don't feel so alone right now. I like that he understands the importance of family. I like that sitting here beside him is so easy.

He tutors me in taking baseball stats, showing me how to draw a thick line from home plate to first base to denote a single. He scratches out the little "1B" next to the thick line. He says that if the ball hits a runner, I have to write BHR across the little field. A double means drawing two dark lines, and if a pitcher hits a batter, I'm supposed to write HBP real big. If a batter hits a homer, I draw four dark lines from base to base to base to home plate, then I denote how many runs get batted in by writing the number of runs and circling it. A bunt is BT.

"I thought BT meant bacon and tomato," I say, and Brian chuckles softly at my stupid joke. Generous of him. I lean so close to watch as he fills out the scorecard, I can feel his breath, warm against my cheek. This is the first time in a long while that an adult has paid a lot of attention to me. Paid attention, and treated me like an equal.

"So, any questions?" Brian asks, snapping the stats book shut. He grabs a glove from a cubby under the bench.

"Yeah, when are practices?"

"Mondays, Tuesdays, Thursdays, and Saturdays, except for when we have games, which are usually on Tuesdays, Thursdays, and Saturdays."

"Darn," I mumble.

"How come? Are you on yearbook staff or in the play or something?"

"I have WNYG on Wednesdays and I was hoping I could get out of it."

"WNYG?"

"Wednesday Night Youth Group at church. Brother John thinks calling it WNYG makes it sound sexy."

Brian snorts. He puts the glove on his left hand and starts breaking it in with his other fist.

I keep blabbering, "Dad makes me go to church, but I can't stand it anymore." Why am I being so honest with this guy?

"Where do you go?"

"Forrest Sanctuary."

He bites at a hangnail. "Huh. That's where my parents go."

"Every Sunday?"

"Every Sunday."

I've never seen him there. And over five hundred people are in the congregation, so I have no idea who his parents are. "But you don't go?"

He stops biting his nail and goes back to pounding his glove. "It's not really my thing either."

"What, you mean you don't love eating stale powdered donuts during Coffee Time in the Fellowship Hall?"

He chuckles.

"Hoffman!" Coach Burns calls from over by third base. "You teaching her the history of baseball or something?"

"We better go," Brian says, standing and adjusting his beige cap. He gives me a nervous smile. I hope he'll put out a hand, to help me stand up, but he doesn't.

Disappointment should be my middle name.

• • •

"Disappointment" can't begin to describe how it felt losing Laura and Allie. Sure, you may have shown me that Laura's not the best friend I've ever had, which is probably better in the long run, but I still feel the loss. No more Saturday nights at the drive-in. No more impromptu fashion shows in Allie's mom's walk-in closet. No more roasting marshmallows over a stove burner.

Written after practice on February 13. Burned.

• • •

I sit Indian style up against the fence beside the third base line, taking stats. I have to admit I'm enjoying it.

Corndog steps up to the plate and taps his bat on the ground three times before getting into his stance. He watches the first pitch smack into the catcher's mitt.

"Strike one," Coach Burns says.

"That was high, Coach!" Corndog yells.

"High my ass!" Sam yells from center field. "I'm a billion feet away and I could tell that was a strike."

"Shut your face, Henry!" Corndog calls.

"I wonder if they'll let me retire tomorrow," Coach Burns replies.

On the next pitch, Corndog sends the ball over the right field wall. He whoops as he rounds the bases. "Yo, Parker! You wrote that down, right?" he calls out as he rounds third. He points at me before crossing home plate, shoving his fists toward the sky, doing the *Rocky* pose.

Does he have to be so perfect at everything? Everyone's been saying he applied to big-time schools like Harvard. I mark his homer, filling in the diamond with pencil.

"Parker Shelton? Is that you?"

I glance up to find a clearly pregnant Coach Lynn standing before me.

"It's me," I reply, deadpan, turning my focus to stats. Drew is the next batter up; I write down his name.

"What are you doing here?" she asks.

"She's our new manager."

I jerk my head up. Brian's hovering beside my former softball coach.

"Manager?" Coach Lynn exclaims. "You told me you'd rather burn in hell than have anything to do with softball ever again. You're willing to manage, but you won't play for me?" She touches her swollen stomach, looking upset. She must be six months along by now.

Brian furrows his eyebrows at me. He tucks his hands in the pockets of his sweatshirt and chomps his gum.

I twirl my pencil.

"Well?" Coach Lynn presses.

I shrug. I've got nothing to say to her.

"You threw away your chance to play in college, Parker. You're about to graduate. I know you love softball."

"She played for you?" Brian asks.

"She was on my varsity squad her freshman and sophomore years. Could've been the best third baseman Hundred Oaks has ever seen."

"Varsity? As a freshman?" Brian blurts.

I lick my lips and glance at his face, then clear my throat. "If you'll excuse me, I need to pay attention to practice." I watch as Drew scoops at a low pitch and misses it. "Stats are very important to Coach Hoffman's decision-making process."

"Decision-making process," Coach Lynn repeats.

"That's right," Brian says. The look on his face shocks me. His

19

dark eyes are questioning, pissed. Wary. He crosses his arms and heads out to center field, to talk to Sam.

"I'd love to have you on the team," Coach Lynn says, rubbing her belly. "Just say the word. You don't have to manage the boys' team if you want to be around the game again."

I shake my head. "That's not it."

I've never told Coach Lynn why I quit after the first practice last season. Softball was something Mom and I shared, and simply slipping a glove on my hand reminded me of how she left. It hurt like hell, but I thought I could handle playing again. But after everything went down with Laura, it sent me over the edge, and I quit. Coach Lynn's tried, unsuccessfully, to get me back. But she doesn't know how it felt, how my own team made fun of me. What happens in the locker room stays in the locker room.

"Our practice starts right after the boys are done," Coach Lynn says. "I'd love to see you there." She waddles off toward the left field equipment shed, where I see my former teammates gathering. That's when Laura and Allie James pass by the fence. Laura has broad shoulders and blonde hair and is much shorter than me or Allie, who's a tall, bony first baseman.

"I can't believe they let *her* be manager," Laura says loudly. "It can't be good for the team's image."

"I wish I got to spend time with all those boys," Allie replies quietly, sounding wistful. They sashay toward the equipment shed.

Laura was the worst after Mom left, after I screamed that her dad was being a jerk and not a very good Christian. She was captain junior year and said, "Don't stare at the other girls in the locker room. I won't stand for it." Why would I want to follow a leader like that?

Some other girls on the team taunted me too, asking questions like, "How do lesbians have sex anyway?" and "You're not gay, right? 'Cause that would just be weird."

Allie took a step back and bit her lip. She looked sympathetic, but ultimately kept hanging out with Laura because her mom worried I'd be a bad influence on her daughter. I never bothered to reach out to Allie after that. I mean, why? So my heart could be broken again?

Still, watching my team pull bats and catching equipment and helmets out of the shed nearly brings me to tears. I don't need them, I tell myself. I've got Drew. The person who didn't judge me.

Brian comes back over, squats beside me, and studies my score-keeping. "Did you already know how to take stats?"

"Yeah," I mumble, fumbling with my pencil.

His brow wrinkles. "I don't appreciate it when people waste my time."

Then he's gone.

stalkerish tendencies aren't necessarily a bad thing, right?

51 days until i turn 18

Practice ends, and after pouring the water onto the grass and storing the coolers in the shed, I go meet Drew in the parking lot. He's standing with Sam, who's gesturing wildly.

"I don't know why Dr. Salter has to approve our prom theme this year," Sam exclaims. "How was I supposed to know that when I suggested a pajama party prom last year a bunch of guys would show up only in their underwear?"

Drew's cracking up. "Um, you wore snakeskin boxers that sparkle, dude."

"Fancy, weren't they?" Sam laughs. "I wear the cutest underpants."

I preferred Chase Neal's puppy dog boxers. I really like animals.

"So if we win the Prom Decisional, what theme will we suggest?" Drew asks Sam.

"I'm thinking we should tell Dr. Salter we want an Ancient Rome theme. We can all show up in togas!"

I smile, tucking my hands in my pockets. Sam's nice and funny, but I don't know him like I know Drew. I usually keep to myself when he hangs out with his friends. And that's fine. I prefer to keep most people at bay.

"I'm glad you're not on the softball team," Sam says to me. "It'd be a lot harder to beat y'all if you were playing."

Every April, the Hundred Oaks softball team plays the baseball team, and whoever wins gets to pick the prom theme. The softball team won my freshman and sophomore years, but lost junior year. A lot of the guys were glad I didn't play. They got their Underpants Prom, after all.

Prom is on May first, but I'm not sure if I'm going. Aside from all the wild underwear, last year wasn't much fun considering Drew and Amy were suctioned together at the mouth the entire time, and my date, He Who Shall Not Be Named (okay, okay—it was Charlie McIntosh), kept trying to feel me up in the middle of the gym. Gross. Anyway, I wouldn't mind going to prom this year if I thought it would be a good time with a guy I really like and trust. A man like Lord Devereaux, the hero in this romance novel I'm reading right now. He's a pioneer of women's rights and gives loans to poor people, all while lusting after Princess Penelope.

God only knows why, but Corndog rides a lawnmower up to me. He pats the seat behind his butt. "Your chariot awaits, Parker."

I avoid his eyes and check my phone. I'm supposed to go shopping with Drew this afternoon and don't have time for another Corndog lecture about how I screw over his friends. As if I don't feel bad enough about my life already.

"Dude, why are you riding a lawnmower?" Sam asks.

"Dad caught me drinking again and took away my truck," Corndog pouts.

"Bullshit," Sam says, folding his arms across his chest, laughing. "You never party."

"Fine, fine," Corndog replies, chuckling. "I've been way bored since grades don't matter anymore and I wanted to see how long it'd take me to get here riding this thing. I've been tweaking the engine to make it go faster."

I smile a little. Since I was named valedictorian, I've been bored too. Like me, Corndog's always loved science. We partnered on projects together until Laura started liking him in middle school.

"It seems like walking would be faster than a lawnmower," I say.

"But it's not nearly as cool!" Corndog retorts.

"Henry! Would you get your ass over here!" Jordan Woods calls from beside Sam's truck. He's letting her drive his truck now? Must be real serious.

"Gotta jet. The ole ball and chain needs me," Sam says. His grin is so bright. He jogs to his truck and pulls her into a passionate kiss.

"Get a room!" Corndog yells at them, then focuses on us.

"We're going shopping at Cool Springs," Drew says, pointing at me with his thumb. "You in?"

"I can't," Corndog replies, glancing at my face. "Dad needs my help today. But thanks for the invite." He tools off on his lawnmower. Wow, it does go fast.

"Corndog's dad had to let their farmhand go," Drew whispers. "I guess money is super tight and demand for their milk and eggs is down."

"That's sad," I say, watching Corndog disappear onto the highway toward the countryside.

"I'm worried about him," Drew says before he and I climb into the bug. He checks his hair in the rearview mirror. "Harry Potter movie marathon tonight?"

I buckle my seatbelt. "You don't have plans with Amy?"

He stops combing his hair. Hesitates. "I broke up with her last night."

I cover my mouth with a hand. "I'm so sorry. Why didn't you tell me?"

"I'm just moving on, all right?"

"Are you okay?"

"Fine, fine." He blushes. "I just want to watch Harry Potter."

"I'm in," I reply.

"Great." He claps his hands together once, looking away from the mirror. "There's something I want to talk to you about."

I fiddle with a tangle of hair. Corndog must've known about the breakup before I did and thought Drew did it because he likes me. But I don't think that's possible. Drew and I spend hours lying in bed together, chatting and watching TV and reading. I've never felt that electric charge between us, telling me he wants to make a move. Drew's the friend who stuck by me through everything. I'm scared for him. I'm scared, that, if what I suspect is true, he'll face the same narrow-mindedness I did.

"What do you want to talk—"

"You wouldn't believe what Steven Reed did at the party I was at last night," Drew interrupts.

"What?"

"You know how he broke his leg ice skating last month and how he has to wear a walking cast?"

"Yeah…"

"So he was like completely trashed out at Miller's, and he was stumbling along the road, pretending to hitchhike. And he fell into a ditch, and he was so drunk he started screaming about how he'd broken his leg. And Marie Baird had to convince him that his leg was already broken."

We laugh as Drew turns the ignition. I watch out the window as

Brian climbs into his red Ford F150. Our eyes meet, but he doesn't acknowledge me. What went wrong? Just an hour ago we were joking around. Is he really that mad about the stats? About me wasting his time? Why didn't I tell him the truth?

I wave as his truck pulls away. He doesn't wave back. And that feeling of belonging, of having someone who understands where I've been, fades.

Brian's left blinker turns on.

"Follow him!" I exclaim.

Drew gapes as we pull out of the parking lot. He doesn't question me. He peels out onto the four-lane, heading into town, trailing behind Brian's truck. Good friends don't question stalkerish tendencies, and well, Drew's a great friend.

"Don't stay right behind him," I squeal.

"He doesn't know it's us."

"Okay, one, he has a rearview mirror. And two, how many people have red VW bugs around here?"

Drew lets off the accelerator and swerves into the left lane. I slap a hand on the window as Brian takes the next right, and we keep on going straight.

"Drew! You lost him!"

"You told me not to stay right behind him!" He clutches the wheel.

"I didn't mean lose him altogether." I throw my hands up in the air.

"I'm sorry," Drew says, giving me a weird look. He narrows his eyes. I rub his shoulder. "It's fine...How about Jiffy Burger for lunch?" His face lights up, and he steps on the gas.

I can't eat the food at JB—too many carbs—but their French fries and cherry Sun Drop make my friend happy. And that's enough for me.

• • •

After lunch and shopping with Drew, I find Dad passed out on the couch with his Bible splayed open across his chest. Piles of architecture and floor plan magazines lay haphazardly on the coffee table, alongside a cup of tea.

It's only 5:00 p.m., but he's snoring up a storm. At forty-two years old, he has a full head of brown hair the color of dark chocolate, and only a few wrinkles. He's very handsome, but you can't tell for the sadness. I press a kiss to his forehead. His eyelids flutter open.

"I'll start dinner in a bit," he says, but I tell him not to worry. I'll take care of it. He whispers he loves me.

"Love you too," I mumble back, but he's falling asleep again already. I can hear music, the beat thumping against the walls of Ryan's room. The drums make the floor vibrate. I slowly walk down the dark hallway past prints of the Beijing National Stadium and the Kansas City Public Library to my room and set my shopping bags on the rug. A knock sounds on my door.

"Come in."

Ryan pokes his head in. His brown hair sticks up every which way and one eye is squinty. "Can you help me with my laundry, Park?"

I sit down on my bed and open my laptop. "Give me a few, 'kay?"

"Sure. Thanks." Ryan shuts the door, leaving me alone.

"You're welcome," I mutter. "It's nice to see you. I'm great, thanks. Laura said mean things about me at practice. The chemistry test yesterday was a real bitch, but I studied hard so I hope I get an A. Thanks for asking, Ryan." I stare at my duvet as I say this, feeling like a crazy loser. I wish my brother would tell me he's proud of me, but I doubt he'll ever care about anyone trying to be their best again.

In high school, Ryan was a perfectionist. Woke up every day at

6:00 a.m. Mom would cook him breakfast and iron the button-down shirts he used to wear, while he went over his homework again. Like me, he made straight As, but he exceeded my accomplishments in so many ways. He was student council president. Lots of girls wanted to date him. He ran the yearbook staff. He played shortstop for the Raiders and was elected homecoming king. He ruled high school, but he couldn't wait for college. He couldn't wait to leave behind the people who didn't take school seriously, the people who partied on weekends and didn't give a crap about their SAT scores. He couldn't wait to study premed at Vanderbilt.

He started falling apart the middle of freshman year, after Mom left, after learning that even at a prestigious college, not everyone was focused like he was. It's like the minute our family disintegrated he finally figured out that reality didn't match his dreams.

My cell rings. The caller ID says it's Mom. I let it go to voice mail, then play it on speaker. I pull my knees to my chest and wrap my arms around my shins while I listen.

"Parker…it's me. Mom. I'd love to chat with you, you know, whenever you have a chance. Your dad told me about Vanderbilt. Congratulations! I'm so proud of you. Theresa and I are doing well. We just got a new puppy. She's a labradoodle! That means she's half Labrador, half poodle. I think we're going to call her Annie. I know how much you love that musical…Okay, well, I'll call again soon. I love you." *Beep.*

I save the message. Just like all the others. I lie down on my bed and focus on the ceiling. Try to shove the loneliness out of my mind. I've always wanted a puppy, but Dad and Ryan are allergic. And now Mom has one—without me.

Sometimes I catch Dad staring at a picture of him and Mom that he keeps in his wallet. Dad says he's forgiven her, but does that mean I have to?

I've only seen her twice in the past year. I miss her, and I want her in my life, but I can't bring myself to tell her. I'm ashamed I never call her. But if people hear about me hanging out with my mom again, I'm afraid it'll wreck my life even more. She ruined my family.

Why did God let this happen to me?

• • •

A few hours later, I go down the street to Drew's double-wide trailer, walk inside without knocking, and head to his room.

His buddies on the football team love calling him Double-wide Drew, insinuating that he is well-endowed. It makes Drew laugh. Double-wides are a luxury, you see. My family's lucky enough to have a three-bedroom house, but it's smack dab behind a laundromat and a fried chicken joint, so you can only imagine the smell. A mix of fabric softener and grease. But besides the terrible odor and the fact we are definitely not in the ritzy section of Franklin where people have swimming pools shaped like guitars, the location rocks. It's only three minutes by bike from school, and I love riding my bike everywhere it can take me.

I knock softly, push Drew's door open, and find him sitting at his desk, typing on his laptop, which is surrounded by his bobble-head collection. He's the only person I know who loves writing in his spare time. When he goes to Middle Tennessee State next year, he's going to study journalism so he can be a sports reporter one day. As much as he loves playing football and baseball, he'll never be good enough to get a scholarship. It's a sore subject because he's worked so hard for so long and could really use the money.

It's only Drew and his mom—his dad left before he was born,

and his mom waitresses at Cracker Barrel like sixty hours a week to make ends meet. I cook dinner for Dad and Ryan every night, so I usually end up making Drew a plate too. I set a bowl of steamed rice and chicken on his bedside table.

"Yo, Drewsky," I say, tiptoeing around sports magazines and several days' worth of discarded newspapers.

He turns and smiles wide, standing up. "Harry Potter movie marathon time!" he says, hugging me. He's wearing a thin gray sweater layered on top of T-shirts. He has the right body to play both running back and second base, short and stocky, but somehow he's rocking the skinny jeans. He's fixed his hair again and doesn't smell like boy (like socks). He smells like lemons.

Everyone is used to Drew dressing up and always looking like a million bucks, because he wants to stand on the Titans sidelines and report for ESPN someday. But I feel like it might be more than that. And I don't want people to judge him like they've judged me. I can only hope that his friends would support him more than mine supported me. Corndog's a good friend to him.

I'm not sure why Corndog's comment about me messing around with his friends bothered me so much today, but it did. I mean, I thought guys like one-night flings. Right? I've only made out with, I dunno, four guys on the basketball team? And how many on the baseball team? Two? I can't believe Paul Briggs announced that I put out, right in front of Brian. What must he think of me?

I slip my boots off while Drew inhales the rice and chicken, because he's always hungry. He turns on *Harry Potter and the Sorcerer's Stone* and flips off the lights. He grabs the big bowl of popcorn he popped and then we stretch out on the bed. I've been saving my calories all day for this popcorn.

"Who's your favorite Harry Potter character?" Drew asks, shoving a handful of popcorn in his mouth.

"Ron. Obviously. You?"

He chews. "Hermione. She's a little sex kitten."

I shove his shoulder, nearly knocking him off the bed. "That's so perverted! She's like ten years old in this movie."

"She's older than me now! How is that perverted?" he says with a laugh.

"Would you rather be Hufflepuff or Slytherin?" I ask, picking my first piece of popcorn. Mmmm, butter.

"Slytherin. I like green more than yellow." He pops a piece in his mouth. "As a house elf, would you rather be responsible for combing Hagrid's beard or washing Snape's greasy hair?"

"Gross! Uh, I'd rather comb the beard because I might find interesting animals or food in there. I might even find mini bottles of butterbeer or something."

We talk during the movie, making fun of Draco's terrible slicked-back hairdo and Hermione being a know-it-all until Oliver Wood comes on the screen.

"He's so hot," I say, groaning. "I want to date a guy with a British accent."

"You? Dating?" He snorggles.

"I'd forget about my no-dating rule for Oliver Wood. Just look at him ride that broom!"

Drew bursts out laughing. "If you absolutely had to date someone who lives in Franklin, or else you'd be eaten by a dragon, who would it be?"

"Brian Hoffman." It pops out and I cover my mouth.

"Coach Hoffman? So that's why you wanted to follow him today?"

When Brian and I were talking, I was smiling and laughing and I felt good. I want to know more about him. I enjoyed joking around and loved making him laugh. I liked what he said...*It's a scary thing to wake up and realize the people you need most aren't nearby anymore...But you keep moving.*

I reply, "What can I say? That boy is hot."

"That *boy* is a *man* but yeah, he's hot."

"You think Coach Hoffman is hot?"

"I can tell which guys are hot and which aren't," he says slowly, looking at the TV. "It's not like it's hard."

I clap my hands. "Okay. Here's a test. Oliver Wood—hot or not?"

"Hot."

"Okay, you pass the test."

"What?" he blurts. "That was a short test."

"Fine, fine," I say, laughing. "Is Paul Briggs hot?"

"Oh, hell no."

"Correct." I tap my lip. "Is Coach Hoffman hot?"

"I believe we've established that. You sure are thinking about him, huh?" He taps the back of my hand.

My face heats up. "Is Corndog hot?"

"It's weird thinking of my friend that way." Drew quickly says, "If you could be any Harry Potter character, who would you be?"

"Professor McGonagall, so I could turn into a cat and sleep all day...If you could have any magical power, what would it be?"

He pauses long enough for Harry to fall in love with the Mirror of Erised. "I'd want to know how people would react ahead of time. To anything, you know?"

"So um, what did you want to talk about? Amy? Why didn't you tell me things weren't okay with her?"

He touches his throat. "Can I get a rain check? I want to watch the movie."

I let out a sigh, relieved, glad he doesn't want to chat.

• • •

Yeah, yeah, Brian probably won't show at church, considering he's never there—trust me, I would've noticed him—but what if he comes today?

I shave everything that needs shaving and moisturize everything that needs moisturizing. I even curl my eyelashes. "Ow," I blurt, when I pull on them too hard. I still haven't gotten the hang of that part of my beauty regimen yet.

I use nail polish remover to ditch the Bubblegum Pink. Then I pull open the top drawer of my vanity and dig through the heap of polishes. Malaysian Mint, Atomic Orange, Blushingham Palace, Canadian Maple Leaf…No, no, no, no.

Brian is older, classier. I bet he'd like a soft color. I paw through the bottles. Going once…going twice…Passion Peach it is. I hum as I redo my nails. Two coats of peach and a layer of clear. I keep messing up my right thumb. I remove the polish twice. Third time's a charm.

I pull on a pink bra, and pinch the skin hanging over the elastic of the matching panties. Brian does not seem like a guy who appreciates muffin top. I drag my hands through my tangled hair, tangling it more.

Last, I put on a sleek black dress and pair it with my leather boots. I've been saving up my baby-sitting money for college, but I decided to treat myself to this dress. I admire it in the mirror, sliding my hands up and down my hips, making sure I look elegant. Not butch. I wince, recalling how Laura told people that.

When I bought the dress at Cool Springs Mall yesterday, Drew said it seemed like a waste of money. "You look hot in anything," he'd said, holding a polo up to his chest, admiring himself in the mirror. "No need to go all Rodeo Drive."

I've got a few minutes before we need to leave for church, so I unzip the dress and lay it carefully on the back of my desk chair. Then I lock my door, lie down on my bed, and slip my fingers under the elastic of my underwear, wondering what it would feel like if a guy touched me there.

I'm praying Brian comes to church with his parents today.

He must've felt the connection too, right?

• • •

Reasons Why I'm the Worst Christian of All Time

Exhibit One: I drop the F-bomb at least twice a day. To tell you the truth, I kinda love the word. It's so versatile. It can be an adjective, a noun, a verb. Also, I take the Lord's name in vain. Sometimes.

Exhibit Two: I break all sorts of Bible rules. I do not treat my body like a temple, like Brother John tells us we should. When Drew snuck wine to school in a Dr. Pepper bottle, I didn't hesitate to take a few sips in the janitor's closet between French III and World History.

Exhibit Three: I don't see how a loving God would split a family up like he did mine. Nor would he mess with Dad's head like that. Brother John always says, "God tests our faith." My question? Why would an all-powerful being be so jealous?

• • •

Church is the one thing Drew won't do with me. Not because he's atheist or belongs to some other religion or cult or anything. He specifically dislikes Forrest Sanctuary. Mostly for how the congregation talked about us after Mom left, but also because the church gives him the heebie-jeebies.

Dad pulls the Durango into the church parking lot. Ryan rubs at his face and the smell of beer and cigarettes and weed sweating out of his body wafts over. If someone gave him a breathalyzer right now, it'd beep louder than a fire alarm. Just call my father Daddy Denial.

Thank heaven our church uses Food Lion grape juice instead of wine at communion, or my brother would probably pass out in front of the altar. Hey, it'd give new meaning to bowing before God. Ryan wouldn't come to church if he had his way, but if he's going to live under Dad's roof, he has to play the game. Ryan *is* a very nice guy. A very nice and always stoned or drunk kind of guy who sometimes gets it on with random girls before Dad comes home. Okay, okay, it's not "random girls." But I'm probably "random" in Macy's eyes. She ignores everything that isn't a really boring book about political science. In that regard, they're a good couple because they are moody and ignore each other for the most part.

I always wear my headphones, to distract myself, when his bedframe slams against the wall between our rooms. I confronted him once, asking why he screws himself over like he does, and he said, "I want to forget." It makes me sad that he wants to get away from the world so bad. I think it's because he's so smart, and sadness comes with knowing so much. I feel sad in that way sometimes.

That's when I see Rachel, Tate, and Aaron waving at me from the church playground. Our parents usually let us hang there instead of subjecting us to Coffee Time before Sunday school. But where's Seth? He's usually attached to Rachel's hip. I think he has a thing for her, but he's too embarrassed to get involved with her, considering the whole scandal with her dad, the district attorney, screwing his secretary and all.

I unbuckle my seatbelt and blurt, "See you at Big Church."

Mom started calling services Big Church when I was little, because the adults went there while kids went to Children's Church. I can't seem to break the habit.

"Bye, Dad!"

"Wait, wait, wait," he says, turning to face me. "You won't miss Sunday school this time, right?"

I rub my palms on my new dress. "It was just that one time. We got to talking about Death Cab for Cutie, and then Laura told us that Brother John believes that any secular music is from the devil! And then Aaron said that at his old church, a bunch of the youth decided to burn all their secular music. Aaron said one girl burned a new iPod. Isn't that fucking outrageous?!"

"Young lady, watch your mouth," Dad replies, glaring at me.

"I don't like you hanging out with all those guys," Ryan says, rubbing his temples with his fingers. "You know what they want, right?"

I shove his shoulder and he groans and leans against the window. His forehead leaves a sweaty smudge on the glass.

"Aren't you cold?" Dad asks me.

"Nope!"

I love that Ryan's bombed *again* and Dad's worried that I'm not wearing a coat. My brother's been getting trashed a lot lately. Sometimes I don't know what to do, like two weeks ago when I came home and found him curled up in bed with an empty bottle of

Robitussin on the floor. He had drunk the whole thing. And when I confronted Dad about Ryan, he asked me to pray with him.

I open the door, step out onto asphalt spotted with overgrown weeds, and make my way to the playground. It's freezing outside, but I can't cover up this rockin' dress.

"Remember what I said about Sunday school!" Dad calls out. "I love you!"

"Love you too!" I yell back.

I skip toward Rachel, Tate, and Aaron, who look me up and down as I approach the seesaw. Aaron's eyes grow wide as he takes in my hips and chest.

"You haven't returned my calls," Aaron says slowly, his eyes becoming narrow slits.

"I'm sorry, I've had a busy week." Now that I know this dress will have the desired effect, I'm ready to go inside to see if Brian's here with his parents.

"You cold?" Aaron asks, slipping his gas station jacket off. Its faded blue linen smells like dust and rain. Last week I buried my face in his shoulder and cringed while he peppered my neck with kisses.

He moves to slide the jacket around my shoulders, but I wave him off. He starts to put his jacket back on, looking disappointed. Corndog's comment about me messing with his friends rings in my mind again. I didn't realize I was hurting guys so much. It never occurred to me that they might want more. Does Aaron actually like *like* me? If so, I feel bad.

"You guys want to get a doughnut?" I ask.

"You? But you never eat anything," Tate says, looking up at me. He's 5'3". He laughs and runs a hand through his shaggy, honey wheat hair. I love how he wears his Converses with black church pants. Leather bands are wrapped around his wrists, and a hemp necklace with a cross charm hangs from his neck. Last week he wore an X-Men tie. I said, "I knew you were a mutant!" and he laughed.

"I love stale powdered doughnuts," I say in a monotone.

"And I'm starving," Rachel adds. She's a sophomore. A younger, tinier version of her brother, Tate. She has a thing for wearing sweet little dresses and ballet flats.

Tate's nose wrinkles. "You actually want to go inside 15 minutes before Sunday school starts?" I see his hand moving inside his pocket, touching something. Must be a cigarette he's dying to light up.

"Please?" I whine.

"Doughnuts for the win," Aaron says, shoving his hands in his pockets.

I whisper to Rachel as we walk. "Do you know a Brian Hoffman? I think his parents go to church with us."

"No, I've never heard of him," she whispers back. "Hey, I love that dress. Goes great with the boots."

I smile. "Thanks. How're things going with Seth? Did he ask you out yet?"

She scrunches up her face. "No. I invited him over Friday night and his parents said he couldn't come, but he snuck out and came anyway. We kissed a couple times, but I don't know what's going on with us."

I give her a sympathetic look. "I'm around if you want to talk or anything."

She smiles and takes off to find Seth. We trudge up to the Fellowship Hall and get in line for Coffee Time. I avoid Mrs. Carmichael, this ninety-something-year-old lady who thinks I'm Sophia Loren. For real. She believes I'm an actress and always tries to touch my face and hair. If she gets hold of my arm, her grandson will have to pry her off me.

Then Laura and Allie strut past, giggling.

"Where does she think she is? A strip club?" Laura says, taking in my outfit.

I don't reply—it's not right to hurt other people's feelings, even if they've hurt mine. I smooth my dress. My eyes water.

"Prudes," Tate says under his breath, making me smile. "Jealous prudes."

That's when Brother John walks by. The youth pastor says, "I hope you haven't been smoking again, Tate. God never intended for you to abuse yourself like that." He scans my dress, and my body tenses up as he stalks off.

"Good morning to you too," Tate says, the corner of his mouth edging up.

I don't know why we still come here, what Dad's trying to prove. I look across the room as he chats with Tim Anderson of Anderson's Paint and Hardware and Jack Taylor of the Jack Taylor Ford dealership. Sometimes I hear them teasing Dad because he works at City Hall, stamping housing permits and whatnot, and doesn't own his own business or have stock or anything. Whatever. He says he comes for "fellowship" and "friends," but what kind of friends don't stick by you after your wife leaves? No one from church ever invites him to bingo parties or to play golf anymore.

So what if he's been coming here since he was a boy? Gramma and Poppy retired to Florida—it's not as if they'd notice if we stopped coming. But Dad's always talking about the good times he's had here, hoping the good times will start again. For years and years, he ran the church-wide barbecue and held barbecue sauce contests. All the men went wild for it. But Brother Michael canceled it last year, claiming interest had gone down. Dad said he understood, but I was so sad for him.

I have a lot of good memories from church too. Pouring hot wax into sand at Vacation Bible School, to make a candle for Mom. Packing baskets of canned goods and delivering them to less privileged families. Kneeling at the altar and thanking God for my friends. For Laura and Allie, who I played Beauty Parlor with. In junior high, we'd go to the city pool, lay our beach towels on the steaming hot concrete, and stare at Jeff, this lifeguard who looked like a Ken doll and drove a Harley.

I get a powdered doughnut and a black coffee, then go stand next to a window where I can see the entire room. Prime vantage point. No sign of Brian. Tate and Aaron join me, holding white paper napkins filled with donuts.

Tate and Aaron eat approximately twenty stale doughnuts and slurp down their coffees in the amount of time it takes me to eat my one doughnut. The church bell dings and dongs, letting us know that Sunday school starts in ten minutes. I love that bell. When I was little, the ushers would let me pull the long velvet cord, to make the bell sound clear across the county. I wish life were still simple like that sound.

It's like the minute we entered high school, the church's messages all changed. It was no longer about loving God. It was about not sinning. No drinking beer, no touching body parts that bathing suits cover, no swearing.

"Why aren't Seth and Rachel hanging out with us?" I ask.

Tate's face goes white. "Well, his mom told him to stop hanging around us…I guess she saw you and Aaron on the playground last Sunday, um…"

Aaron crumples his Styrofoam cup. "Shut up, man."

I stare across the Fellowship Hall at Seth. He lifts his chin, acknowledging me, then goes back to talking to Rachel. Seth's mom doesn't seem pleased about that either. I get that his mom wants to protect him. But Rachel's a sweet girl.

I used to be a sweet girl.

Tate and Rachel didn't turn on me post Mom-gate. They go to Woodbury High, with Aaron, so it's not like we're great friends or anything, but they're good company. We giggle a lot. Especially when Brother John does PowerPoint presentations of common devil worshipping signs.

But Aaron's new here. That's the only reason his parents haven't told him to steer clear of me, Parker Shelton, Sinner Extraordinaire.

I should have business cards made.

• • •

They say you give us gifts. You made Drew great at football, but he's no Jordan Woods. He'll never play in college. You made Dad an architect, but he's not designing skyscrapers in New York or opera houses in Paris. You made me into a killer softball player. Good enough to make the all-conference team sophomore year. But more than that, you gave me something I loved.

But didn't you realize that when you took Mom from me, that you were also taking something we shared? Mom was there the first time I picked up a tee-ball bat. Mom bought me my first glove. She showed me how to put a ball in my glove, wrap it up in a rubber band and put it under my pillow at night, so I could break it in. So I could dream about it.

But you took away that dream, and now I don't know what's left.

Written during services on February 14. Burned.

• • •

Brian never showed at Big Church.

But before I left, I lifted a copy of the church directory from the main office, so I could stalk Brian in the comfort of my home.

"Is that them, you think?" Drew asks, pointing at a picture of an older couple. The caption reads Mr. and Mrs. William Hoffman. Where Brian's sexiness came from is not evident in this picture. But they're the only Hoffmans at Forrest Sanctuary.

I close the directory, go over to my vanity, and drag a hand through my drawer o'nail polishes. I pick out Bodacious Boysenberry and carry it to my bed, where I plop down next to Drew and start removing Passion Peach.

"Let's Google him!" he says, opening my laptop, going into reporter mode.

I groan. If I do that, I'll be a bona fide stalker. My business card should actually read "Parker Shelton, Slutty Sinner Sleuth Extraordinaire."

Drew's already typing his name into the search bar. Right then Ryan pokes his head in my room.

"Are you hungry?" he asks. Dark circles ring his eyes.

"Give me twenty minutes, and I'll start cooking," I say, holding up my nails. Ryan nods and the door clicks shut. I love, love, love cooking, but it's the only chore I really like. I love taste testing. Mom never worked. She was a housewife, and when she left, I had to take on chores like laundry and ironing after Dad turned his T-shirts pink and burned his thumb while pressing his pants. I wish Mom and Dad were still together. I wish her dog Annie was here. All I really want in life is a big furry dog that slobbers a lot.

"Here he is!" Drew says. Brian's Facebook page pops up. The profile picture is of him in a Georgia Tech baseball uniform, holding a bat. He's smiling. He's younger than he is now. The rest of the profile is locked down, so I can't get any juicy details like his favorite books and movies, to see what we have in common.

"You should friend request him," Drew says, moving the cursor to click the button.

"No way!" I slap his hand and log out of my account before he does something drastic.

I make a split-second decision to repaint my nails with Passion Peach.

When I asked if he played ball, Brian replied, "Something like that." He played college ball but won't admit it?! I start to Google his name, then shut the laptop. I will not be a psycho, no matter how much I want to know him. No matter how much I want to feel that link again. He understands what it's like to miss someone. He treated me like I'm somebody worth knowing.

Brian Hoffman. Who are you?

defcon 1

My Monday thus far:

1. Ride bike to school. Store bike at racks. Notice Brian's red truck. Casually peek in windows for clues as to who he is. A fruit punch Gatorade sits in the center console along with a heap of coins. He has two bumper stickers: one is for the Braves, the other reads COEXIST and is covered by all these symbols that I recognize from Brother John's PowerPoint presentation on devil worshipping signs. Based on this evidence, I have determined Brian and I are meant to be together. I love Gatorade! I use money! The Braves were my team once. I believe in coexisting. Totally meant to be together! (Kidding, kidding.)

2. Inside Hundred Oaks before first period, I make a point of walking by Coach Burns's office near the gym. No sign of Brian. Unfortunately I hear Coach Burns talking on his phone. His sweet nothings are gag-worthy. "Yes, baby. I love you, sweet plum." Sweet plum? Really?

3. Daydream during advanced US history. Does Brian have

an apartment? I picture myself tangled up in his crumpled sheets, our legs knotted. The idea scares me a little because I've never gotten naked with anybody. I close my eyes, thinking of him in the buff, and accidently let out a moan. The entire class looks at me.

Silence.

Crickets.

Embarrassment.

"Slut," Laura hisses under her breath.

Prude, I think, remembering what Tate said at church.

"Hey, hey! I'm trying to learn here," Sam says, slipping a pencil behind his ear. "Some of us think about more than the opposite sex."

"No one believes that, Sam," Mr. Davis says, rubbing his eyes.

4. I walk by Coach Burns's office between classes. Where is Brian? He must be the only coach/teacher who doesn't actually come to school. *Gar.* This time Coach Burns has two guys in his office and is yelling at them for horsing around in the locker room. Apparently one guy stole the other's clothes and tried to flush them down the toilet, which explains why the other is wearing only boxers with pine trees on them. I remember those boring underpants from the Pajama Party Prom.

• • •

At lunchtime, I'm sitting in the cafeteria, checking over Drew's algebra, when Corndog plops down next to me.

"Can I see your calc homework?" he asks. "I want to make sure I got the third word problem right."

A month ago, I would've said "hells to the no," but valedictorian is in the bag and Corndog got stuck in second place because he bombed that horrific chemistry pop quiz back in October. Ha! Our school announced the valedictorian and salutatorian in January, so I'm not studying for three hours a night anymore.

"Which problem was that again?" I ask.

Corndog reads from his book. "A cup is in the shape of a truncated cone with a radius of 4 centimeters at the top and 2 centimeters at the bottom and a height of 6 centimeters. Water is being poured into the cup such that the height of the water in the cup is changing. Write an equation for volume of the water in the cup as a function of its height."

"That one was hard. My answer's in my blue folder." I nod at my backpack. He digs around inside, pulls out the folder, and brushes his brown hair away from his face.

I erase Drew's answer to number four and fill in the correct one. He hovers over my shoulder, watching.

"Ohhh," he says.

"Are y'all cheating?" Corndog asks, peering at Drew's homework.

"No." I feel myself blushing. "What do you think you're doing?" I ask, pointing at my paper.

"The only reason I couldn't do this problem is 'cause I didn't have a cup." Corndog purses his lips, laughing.

I set my pencil down. "Enlighten me."

"Don't you have my cup? As manager of the baseball team, aren't you in charge of our equipment?"

Drew bursts out laughing.

"I am *not* in charge of your cups or your dirty jockstraps."

"Tsk tsk. I'm going to report you to Coach Hoffman for not being in complete control of our equipment."

Drew is wiping tears away from his eyes.

I stare Corndog down. "I'm going to report you for being a complete tool."

"How am I supposed to write an answer to this problem if you can't tell me where my cup is?"

"There's no way in hell I'd touch a cup."

"Not even say, Bates's?" He smirks and stares past me at Drew, who quickly looks away. His face goes red, and he plucks his algebra homework from my hand, gathers his backpack and laptop case and storms out of the cafeteria.

"What was that about?" Corndog asks, his forehead crinkling.

I rap my pencil on the table. "Piss off, Corndog."

"Whoa." His face turns serious. "What's wrong?"

"On Saturday…you said something about Drew? Did you really think I'd use my best friend? Do you really think I'm that kind of person?" I play with a string hanging from my hoodie, waiting for him to respond.

He steals a chip off my tray. "On Friday night at Miller's Hollow, he told me he was dumping Amy. He said he doesn't like her as much as he likes someone else."

"And you think he meant me?"

He shrugs and eats another of my chips. "I dunno. I figured so."

I shove a bunch of chips in my mouth and crunch on them. I swallow, hating that I'm giving in to hunger. I want people to see me as pretty, as ladylike.

"I don't like him like that," I say quietly.

"Shit," he replies, dragging a hand through his hair. "Poor Bates." For as much as he gets on my nerves, Corndog's a pretty good friend to lots of people. But he obviously doesn't share my suspicions about Drew.

At the table behind us, Laura is going on and on about the Prom Decisional. "Y'all, you have to vote for a Disney theme. You just have to. I'm gonna dress as Princess Jasmine and I'll get Aaron Pritchard to go as Aladdin!"

Aaron from church? The Aaron I made out with? Same ole Laura. What's mine is hers, and what's hers will always be hers.

"I'd rather do the Roaring Twenties," Allie tells Laura. "Wouldn't flapper dresses be so cute?"

"We're doing Disney!" Laura squeals.

Corndog groans so low I can barely hear him. "Disney sounds terrible."

"I like Ancient Rome more," I reply. "I have this gorgeous white silk dress I could wear." It belonged to Mom, but she never wore it and left it behind for me.

"Sounds pretty. Who are you going with?"

"No one in particular. I love my dress though," I say, smiling to myself.

"I'm thinking of suggesting a Ho Down Prom. We'll tell all the girls it's a farm theme, you see, but really all the guys will dress in drag. Like hookers. Get it? A Ho Down?"

I laugh. "I'd pay money to see that."

"Right?" Corndog chuckles and grabs another chip. "So are you gonna tell me what you did with my cup?"

I grab a handful of chips and throw them in Corndog's face.

I hear a laugh. A shadow falls across my tray and papers, and someone taps my shoulder. "Parker, I'm glad to see you're keeping my captain in check."

I twirl around and look up to find Brian Hoffman standing there in a button-down Oxford shirt and black tie. He looks like a Geek Squad sexpot. Black hair falls in waves around his ears.

He nods once at me. "I need your help with something after practice this evening. Can you stay for fifteen minutes or so past six o'clock?"

"Fifteen minutes?" I squeak.

"Give or take a few." Brian smiles.

I examine my nail polish. I'm glad I stuck with Passion Peach. "Yeah, I can do that."

"Okay, see you then."

A bunch of girls, including Laura, stare at him as he struts out of the cafeteria.

Corndog gives me a smile and looks from me to the cafeteria doors, shaking his head. "You are highly entertaining, Parker Shelton."

• • •

You're not going to believe this, but after lunch, I don't stalk Coach Burns's office to look for Brian. Instead, I stalk Drew's locker to make sure he's all right. A sign advertising the annual Baseball-Softball Prom Decisional on April third hangs on the wall. Tickets for the game are already on sale.

I glance at my watch a few times and slide on fresh lip gloss while waiting for him. Approaching at my ten o'clock is Ty Green, aka the hottest guy at school, swaggering sexily. We talked briefly at this New Year's party, but he disappeared before the ball dropped. When the ball fell, I was all alone, and this incredible loneliness washed over me, like being pulled under by a strong tide.

Ty gives me this knowing grin, then heads toward the art room. That's when Drew shows up with Matt Higgins, who does this vanishing act into the library. As if he's ever been in there.

Drew opens his locker to check his reflection in the little mirror he has hanging inside.

"Hey," I say quietly. "Can we talk?"

"I'm busy."

"You look fine."

"Yeah?" He grins at himself in the mirror.

"You're like the Narcissus of Hundred Oaks."

He looks over his shoulder at me. "Who? You callin' me a girl?"

I shut my eyes and shake my head. My brother has been complaining for years that he and I must be the only cultured people in Franklin. "No, he was this Greek guy. In the time of the gods."

"You think I'm a Greek god? I knew you loved me."

"Come on, you." I shut his locker door and pull him into the library, leading him to the magazine room. We fall down onto cushy chairs. Drew sets his laptop case on the floor. He always keeps his computer nearby in case he has a free moment to write.

I open my purse and pull out my compact so I can re-powder my face. I dab it across my nose and chin. "Are you okay?"

"Fine." He props his ankle on his knee and shakes his foot.

"You ran out of the cafeteria. I was worried." I shut my compact and slip it back into my bag.

Drew drums his fingers on the chair's arm, then takes my hand and studies my peach nails. "I like this color. It's simple." He slowly meets my eyes.

My cell beeps, and I quickly check the screen. Mom. She sent me a text saying she hopes I'm having a nice day. "Ugghhh," I groan. "She's so annoying. She won't let go."

"Who was that?"

"Mom."

"Have you talked to her lately?" Drew asks softly.

"No."

"Sometimes she calls my mom to check in, because you never answer her calls. Why haven't you?"

"Because," I snap. The librarian gives me a warning glare. "She ruined my family and everything with my church when she…you know…came out. I just don't get why she had to leave us."

I rarely talk about any of this, not even with my family, so I'm surprised it's tumbling out of my mouth. It's like, if none of this had happened, everything would've been okay with me—with church, with softball, maybe I would've had real dates. The real goddamn kicker is that her girlfriend, Theresa, was the church office assistant.

"But it's not your mom's fault," Drew starts.

"But it is." I shove the phone deep in my bag.

"She can't help it—"

"It doesn't bother me that she's gay. I just wish my family was still together." My eyes water.

He hesitates, and looks around the magazine room. His mouth opens, but the warning bell rings for next class and Drew jumps to his feet. He throws an arm around me as we enter the crowded hallway.

• • •

Laura had a big black dog named June. I loved going to her house. I'd throw stick after stick, and June would go retrieve them and lope back to me, and I swear, if dogs could smile, June would have the biggest grin on her face. I loved playing with that dog. Hugging her. Kissing her. Laura hated that I got along so well with the dog, because June belonged to her and she didn't like sharing.

Then, one Sunday morning, Laura told me June had died. I cried during Sunday School. I wiped tears off my face during Big Church, using the hem of my dress. Mom and Dad asked what was wrong, so I told them the dog had died. When my parents expressed their condolences to Brother John, he told them June was alive and well. And then Brother John gave me a lecture on how lying is a straight path to Hell. I never told anyone that Laura lied. I didn't want anyone to tell her she was on a path to Hell.

Written February 15. Wadded up and burned. The flame caught my thumb and I stuck it in my mouth, to soothe it.

• • •

Today's practice starts out with a team meeting. I squeeze between Drew and Sam on the bleachers.

Brian is standing in front of us, twirling a bat in his hands like a pinwheel. I'm glad to see he ditched the Best Buy employee costume for a sweatshirt and baseball pants that've seen a few workouts.

He glances at me and then focuses on Coach Burns, who clears his throat and reads from his clipboard, telling us about the first game set to take place Saturday against Tullahoma. He explains that we should meet at school at 6:30 a.m. to get on the bus so we can go to Cracker Barrel for breakfast and then make it to Tullahoma in time to warm up.

Drew growls, "I hate Cracker Barrel. I'm sick of it." His mom is always bringing food home because she gets a 50 percent discount.

"I love their pancakes," I say, knocking my knee against his. "I wish you'd hook me up more often."

Drew knocks his knee against mine. "As if you'd eat a pancake."

"I would eat one."

"Pancakes or waffles?"

"Waffles. Syrup or butter?"

"Miss Shelton, is there a problem?" Brian asks. He stops twirling his bat.

"Um, no?" I narrow my eyes at him.

"No private conversations while Coach Burns is talking, please." He turns his gaze from me to Coach Burns, and heat rushes through my body. Why'd he have to embarrass me like that?

Since the softball team is still using the field, Coach Burns starts talking strategy for Tullahoma, the first of forty-five games. The football team gets all the money they want, but our baseball and softball teams share equipment and a field. Coach Burns seems like the kind of guy who makes do with whatever he gets. What kind of coach will Brian be next year?

Coach Burns says *blah, blah* and I focus on the softball team, watching them scrimmage. The girl they've got playing third base has poor range. She's not quick on her feet. I could always cover the entire gap between third and shortstop, diving when I needed to, taking a ball straight to the gut when required. This girl barely moves three feet, then lets the left fielder clean up her mistakes.

Laura steps up to bat next. I feel a pang of hatred for her as I watch her dig a trench with her cleat. She taps her bat on home plate then rests it on her shoulder. Terrible stance. How is Coach Lynn standing for this?

I scan the field for her, but she's nowhere. Then I notice Mr. Majors, the music teacher, is standing by the dugout reading *People*. What? Where's Coach Lynn? They've got the resident accordion player *supervising* practice? Huh. I hope she's okay.

Laura swings at the first two pitches, missing both.

I pull my knees to my chest and stare at the field, sort of wishing I was out there. Ever since I came here on Saturday, my hands have been aching to hold a bat. I want to slip cleats on and jog the bases and slide into home. I shake these ideas out of my head the moment I see Allie and Melanie pointing at me from first and second bases, respectively.

Boy, have I fallen. I might as well be third-string.

Laura takes a few more practice swings. Hardly any pitchers are great batters, because they spend all their time practicing pitching, but Laura's worse at bat than most. She makes up for it on the mound—she's one of the best in the conference. I'm feeling evil, so I pray she'll strike out. *Strike out, strike out.* She steps up and swings away at a high ball.

Strike three!

I clap my hands together and laugh.

"Is there something you'd like to share with us, Parker?" Brian asks.

"No, *sir.*"

He gives me a look. He mouths, *sir?*

I salute, which makes him chuckle. His eyes look like melted Hershey's Kisses.

I can't wait to find out what he needs help with after practice.

• • •

An eon later, practice ends.

Brian beckons me to follow him toward center field, toward the batting cages. He twirls his bat and glances back at me.

I trot up to his side. "So you need my help with something?"

"I do." His stride is long and full of importance.

I pull my hair over one shoulder and play with a clump of it, trying to de-stress. He smells delicious, like bubblegum, and his frayed sweatshirt looks soft. It's the kind of shirt I'd love to curl up in to watch TV.

"Have you ever had a haircut?" he jokes.

"Not in a while."

"Hmmm." He checks my tangles out.

"I like my hair! Most guys like it too!"

He laughs and chews his gum, making a smacking noise. "I didn't say I don't like it."

"Right. You didn't say anything."

"Nothing to say." He goes silent. Cars roar by on the highway beyond the train tracks.

"I'm sorry I wasn't totally honest with you about the stats on Saturday…It's just, I was enjoying talking to you and didn't want to stop."

He nods and gives me a smile. "Apology accepted."

He pulls open the center field gate, and we walk over to the batting cages. The sun has completely set, and only a few floodlights illuminate the field. I shiver, and warm my hands in my armpits.

"You cold?" he asks.

I nod. Normally, this is when the guy would warm me up in some way, by hugging me or giving me his jacket or starting an intense make-out session that would leave me hotter than a volcano. But all Brian does is turn on the pitching machine and swing his bat.

"You want me to load balls for you?" I ask, not totally disappointed. It's nice he wants my company.

He finds my eyes. "No. I want you to hit for me."

My mouth falls open. My fingers itch to hold a bat. My fingers itch to hold him too, but that's beside the point.

I step closer and look up at his face. "Why?"

"Uh…I'm interested to see what you've got. You played varsity as a freshman? That's gotta mean something."

I shrug.

"Will you hit a few balls? For me?" His voice is soft and pleading.

"What's it to you?"

He moves a step closer and stares down at me. "I'd hate to see someone with potential throw it all away."

"If I bat for you, what's in it for me?"

He smirks slightly. "What do you want?"

You. I don't say that though. He watches as I play with my hair.

"In return, I want you to tell me about what baseball means to you," I say. "Did you play? And you can't just say 'something like that.'"

He exhales, and stares up at the stars. "Yes, I played. Now you have to hit a ball."

I grab his elbow. "That's not good enough. Where did you play? For how long? What position? What's your best batting average? Or are you a pitcher? What's your ERA?"

"Whoa, whoa, whoa," he says, raising a hand, looking amused. "Bat first, talk second."

I take the aluminum bat from his hand, run my fingers over the cool metal, and take a few practice swings. My arms feel stiff and weak, but I haven't lost my mechanics. Batting is like breathing.

He steps over to the pitching machine and turns it off. The whirring sound ceases. He picks up a softball and tosses it to himself. "I'll throw a few at you first, if you'd rather."

"Would you turn the damned machine back on?"

He raises his eyebrows, smiles, and laughs. "You're a feisty one. No wonder all the guys like you so much."

I shoot him a look, but deep down I'm pleased he called me feisty and knows that guys like me. One point for Parker.

He turns the machine back on and stands behind the protective fence. I put on a batting helmet.

"Ready?" he asks.

"Yup." I take another practice swing.

"You've got good form."

"I know."

He grins. "Boy, are you humble. Here we go." He feeds a ball into the machine and it whizzes toward me. I let it pass. I dig my boot into the dirt, wishing I had cleats. I take another practice swing.

"Again," Brian says, dropping a ball into the hole.

This time I swing and make contact. The ball slams into the fence right in Brian's face.

"Sure. Take whatever's wrong out on me," he says with a smile.

"That's the plan." Back into my stance. Practice swing before the real thing. This time I connect. Feel a rush of electricity tingle down my biceps and forearms. I knocked it out of the park. Well, I hit the rear nets. But I bet it would've been out of the park. And it feels *good*. I grin.

"Ready?" Brian asks, holding up another ball.

"Wait." I drop the bat. "You got any more of that gum?"

• • •

At 7:00 p.m.—way past the 15 minutes I'd agreed to—Brian turns off the pitching machine. I only missed, I dunno, six or seven balls out of a hundred? My muscles are screaming at me and I'm stiff as stale licorice, but my mind feels clearer than it has in a long time.

"Damn, you've got a bat on you," he exclaims, walking over as I pull off my helmet. "Fun?"

"It was," I admit. "Now what about my questions? Are you going to answer them now?"

My stomach grumbles.

"Hungry?" He takes his cap off, smoothes his hair, and puts it back on.

"Starved." I poke him in the chest. "But you owe me a bunch of answers."

"True, true." He hesitates. "Would you…"

"Would I?" I'm bouncing on my tiptoes now.

He secures his bat beneath his arm. "Want to get some food?"

Holy scandal!

"What kind of food?" I ask, calm and cool.

"I dunno, does it matter?"

"I don't eat olives."

He chuckles. "I once read that there's an olive in the world for everybody, you just have to find it."

"I haven't found any olives that I like."

"So we won't get olives."

I blow warm air onto my hands and rub them together. "Is this okay? I mean, are we allowed to talk off school property?"

He thinks for a few secs. "I haven't read the school handbook. I have no idea. But we're not going clubbing or anything. We're just getting food, right?"

"Right." Totally cool. I'm totally cool. Breathe. "Why do you want to get dinner with me?"

He lifts a shoulder, chewing his gum. "We both gotta eat."

"Don't you have plans? A family? A girlfriend? A wife?"

He laughs and jingles his keys. "Let's go."

• • •

"This place is a total swamp."

Brian tosses his beige cap onto the dashboard. "I came here all the time in high school."

59

"When? Like fifty years ago?"

"Oh, hush," he says with a smile. He musses his wavy black curls before we climb out of his truck. The neon Foothills Diner sign flickers in the window. Empty plastic bottles and cigarette butts litter the parking lot. No one from school ever comes here—*because* it's a total swamp, making it an ideal place where no one will see us.

He opens the door for me; the little bell jingles. Burger stench hits me in the face.

"This is one of my favorite places."

"Why?" I ask.

"Killer cheese fries." He points at me. "With bacon bits."

My mouth waters. "I loooooooovvve bacon bits."

If Brian wants me to eat cheese fries, I'm eating cheese fries. I once read that the bloomin' onion at Outback Steakhouse has 1,800 calories, so I can only imagine how much fat these cheese fries have. How big are the portions? I take a quick glance around the tiny diner and find that the plates are the size of trashcan lids. *Lovely.*

Brian asks the hostess if we can take the booth in the corner, and a wave of embarrassment floods my body. He doesn't want to be seen with me. But if he didn't want to be seen with me, would he risk going anywhere public? Believe it or not, swampy Foothills Diner is a public place.

"Parker?"

I look up to find Brian already sitting in the booth with his arm stretched across the back of the seat, and I'm still standing by the door. I'm such a nerd. I shuffle over and plop down in the seat across from him right as the waitress saunters up to ask for our drink order. She checks Brian out the way I stare at pictures of cupcakes.

Brian reads the drink menu. "I'll take a PBR on tap."

He ordered a beer?! He's a coach at my school and he orders a beer? What does that mean? Does he feel comfortable with me like I feel comfortable with him?

"And for you?" the waitress asks, giving me stink eye. It's like she's daring me to order a beer.

I take the menu from Brian's hand and scan it. My fingers stick to the sticky plastic. "Iced tea? Unsweetened."

"Coming up," the waitress says, smiling brightly at Brian, and then goes behind the counter.

"I forgot you can't drink yet," he says.

"I can't even vote yet."

He examines the mini jukebox on the table. "When can you?"

"April fifth."

He rubs the scruff on his jaw. "So you've got a great bat. I can't wait to see you in the field."

"Who says you're going to see me in the field?" I start looking over the dinner menu, to see if anything might be less than 80,000 calories.

"I figured…You know, since you enjoyed batting tonight, you might want to go out for the team again."

The waitress sets our drinks on the table.

"I don't know that I want to rejoin the team, but I do love soft-ball," I admit.

He rushes to sip his beer. "What happened?"

I fish a Splenda out of the sugar caddy, rip the package open, and stir the powder into my tea. "I'm not answering any of your questions until you answer mine, Brian Hoffman. You must be the king of deflection."

"That's me." He shrugs a little, smiling. It's cute, and I find myself leaning across the table toward him, cradling my tea glass with both hands.

"Tell me about you and baseball."

He nurses his beer. "Not much to tell."

"Not much?"

He swallows another sip. "I got a scholarship to play at Georgia Tech, but I never got much playing time."

"What's your position?"

"Right field."

"You must be a great hitter, then."

"I was," he says softly. I get what he means: Playing outfield doesn't take the kind of skill you need to play say, pitcher, catcher, or shortstop. All the really great batters play outfield.

"And then what happened?"

Half his beer is gone already. Will I have to drive him home?

"Lost my timing...wasn't as good as I thought I was...coaches thought I'd peak, but I never did." His brown eyes bore into mine. Embarrassed, but open. My mind flashes back to how he showed me his bitten fingernails.

"Then what happened?" I whisper.

He raps his fork on the table. "In four years of college, I never started. I became a utility player they used only when another guy needed a break."

"Do you regret playing in college?"

"No...it's just, I learned from it. That and...well, I learned that I can't plan anything anymore." He rubs his eyes and looks out the window, hesitating. A semi pulls into the parking lot. "I need to take it all as it comes."

"Aren't some plans important, though?" I ask, thinking of Vanderbilt, where I can start all over.

He shakes his head. "I live for now. Which is why I want to see you play again. I can tell how much you like it. What if you regret it later?"

I lick my lips. He's right. But I'm not sure I want to reach out again.

That's when Waitress Seductress Extraordinaire comes back and gets our order. Brian surprises me by ordering for us. "We're sharing an order of Fries à la Appalachia," he says, handing over the menus and turning his focus back to me. Le waitress stomps off.

I ask, "Why are they called that?"

"Because when they've got the fries stacked up they're higher than a mountain range."

I groan and touch my stomach.

"You're funny," he says, his eyes twinkling. He scrunches his bangs in his fist.

I pull my legs up under my butt and ask, "So do you know which gym class you're teaching yet?"

"Right now I'm shadowing Coach Burns…but I'm going to take over Coach Lynn's classes when she goes on maternity leave the last week of April."

"You're gonna be my gym teacher? You'd better not make us do step aerobics or play with the giant parachute or anything."

"We're definitely gonna play with the giant parachute…" He runs a hand over his head, looking around the diner. He smiles and focuses on me again. "Technically, I'll only be your gym teacher for like two weeks. And then you graduate. And then I'm teaching driver's ed this summer."

"Whoa, that's so cool," I tease.

He laughs, but then grows serious again. "I never planned on becoming a teacher."

"What did you plan on?"

"Going to the majors…And if not that, then maybe working for an MLB club. As a coach or trainer or something. That's why I got a master's, so I could at least work in the game…I might try to get a job doing field crew somewhere. I don't know what I'm gonna do."

I sip my tea and swallow. He doesn't offer any further details about his career choices, so I change the subject. "So, what brought you back here?"

He hesitates and chooses a song to play on the jukebox. "Everywhere" by Tim McGraw. A great, depressing choice. Finally he whispers, "I wanted to be back with my parents for a while?" He says it like a question. Like he's unsure of why he's living with his parents? Like he's unsure of why he's admitting this to me?

Maybe I do need to Google him. Brian Hoffman is like an onion. I peel back one layer only to find a hundred denser layers full of secrets.

"Did you miss your parents?" I ask, missing my own mom like crazy.

He nods, finding my eyes. He looks younger than twenty-three right now. Did he wander after not making it to the major leagues? Is he lost?

"Do you like coaching at all?"

He looks at me over the top of his glass as he sips his beer. "I don't have much interest in writing daily status reports for Dr. Salter on how the baseball team is doing. Shouldn't our win-loss record be report enough? And you wouldn't believe what the women talk about in the teachers' lounge. I've learned all about breast pumps." He shudders.

I laugh. "So it's not what you expected?"

"No." He laughs with me. "I guess I thought…I guess I thought that if I came back to Franklin, I would feel good again. Like in high school."

"College was really that bad?"

"It wasn't what I expected. Like I said, I thought I'd be playing ball and going on to bigger things. I thought if I came back here I could at least have fun with my old friends…but they're all busy planning weddings and buying houses and having kids, and I don't think I'm ready for that."

This conversation feels very adult-ish and mature. I'm glad he's speaking to me about it, but I can tell he doesn't want to. "Okay, on to a more important question," I ask, propping my chin on my fist.

He glances up, wary.

"What's your most embarrassing moment?"

"What?" He looks amused. "That's your important question?"

"It's very important!" I nod seriously, trying not to crack up.

"Okay, well, if I tell you this, you can't tell anyone at school. Understand?"

"Pinky swear." I link my finger with his.

"So…in high school, this buddy of mine and I discovered that if you climbed up on top of the lockers in the boys' locker room, you could push the ceiling tiles up and crawl into the ceiling next to the girls' locker room."

"So you like, fell through the ceiling?"

"I didn't fall through the ceiling! At least…not then anyway."

I laugh. "I gotta hear more."

"Up in the ceiling, the wall between the two locker rooms was made of concrete."

"Concrete."

"My friend Evan got this idea that we could chisel through the concrete. Like make a tunnel."

I laugh.

"We spent two months chiseling through the concrete."

"Weren't you worried about structural damage? Why didn't you just run into the locker room or something if you wanted to see the girls so bad?"

"I was sixteen. I wasn't thinking about structural damage. I was thinking about how if Evan and I ran in the locker room all the girls would scream and yell."

"I'm sure you were hot in high school. Why'd you need to spy on girls to see them naked?"

I cannot. Believe. I said that.

Brian's face goes redder than the ketchup. "That's beside the point."

"Oh really?"

"It was about the adventure!"

"The adventure of chiseling through concrete to spy on girls?" I snorggle.

He gives me a look. "Do you want to hear the rest of the story?"

"Yes."

"Then behave."

I salute. "Yes, sir."

"Would you stop calling me that?"

"Tell the story already."

Our drinks sit untouched as Brian and I move closer and closer, leaning across the table toward each other. We're laughing as Brian goes on to explain that after they chiseled through the concrete, he edged onto the ceiling tiles on the other side, they couldn't support his weight, and he fell straight down into the locker room. Girls wearing nothing but bras and panties ran screaming while he sprained his wrist and got suspended for a week.

"Now I get to ask you an important question," he says, once I'm done wiping tears of laughter off my face. "What's your earliest memory?" he asks.

The Waitrix brings the cheese fries, and we dive in. He invited me out, so screw the calories. I nod, I listen, I ask him questions, I laugh.

To be here with me—a seventeen-year-old, and having a great time, he must truly be living in the now. And so am I.

• • •

It's not my earliest memory, but it's my favorite.

When I was eleven, I packed up my suitcase and went to sleep-away camp for the first time. Cumberland Creek church camp. Laura and Allie went too. We spent the week canoeing and cooking burgers over a crackling campfire and doing three-legged races in Field Olympics. I spent a lot of time in this outdoor chapel, praying and writing in my journal about how much fun I was having and how I loved being a Christian because it made me feel good about myself. I liked being a good person.

During night devotion, the counselors allowed us to write prayers on slips of paper and burn them, so whatever we prayed for would be just between us and Him. I hoped for things like relief for Gramma's arthritis and for Dad and Ryan to stop being allergic to animals so my parents would let me adopt a yellow lab puppy already.

Campers received mail, but if you received more than three pieces of mail, you had to sing a song in front of the entire camp. On Wednesday, I sang "Twinkle, Twinkle" in front of three hundred kids. But I didn't care. My parents loved me enough to send fifteen postcards.

That's my favorite memory.

On the last night of camp, a dance took place and everyone could bring dates. Nobody asked Laura and Allie, and they felt disappointed because that was the activity we'd been looking forward to most. This boy J. C. and I went together and held hands. I'd never done that before. At the end of the night, he kissed my cheek.

I never saw the boy again because he was from Nashville, but Laura and Allie saw the kiss, and I saw the envy in their eyes. Laura told me that I was moving too fast and should be careful or I would end up pregnant, or worse, I would sin. After that, I worried what other girls thought of me. I knew how pretty I was, I knew that boys liked me. But I didn't so much as hold hands with another guy until after Mom left. Up until then, I'd never done anything wrong, never even kissed a boy on the lips. But my church turned on me anyway.

• • •

Brian pulls his truck up to my house.

He peers at my yard. I hope he's not disgusted by the stench of fried chicken and laundromat. "This is it?"

"This is it."

We sit in silence for a minute, listening to the Fray. This silence isn't awkward. It's nice, and I probably should get out of the truck, but I don't want to. Not yet.

"So will you think about playing ball this year?" he asks quietly, drumming his fingers on the steering wheel.

Ever since Corndog asked me to stay away from Drew, I've been thinking about my reputation. How even though I've never made a move on Drew, Corndog thought I might, which goes to show that even if my intentions are good, someone could misinterpret them.

If someone saw Brian and me at Foothills Diner tonight, they might've thought:

1. He's my big brother. (Ew.)
2. He's my husband. (Kinda weird.)
3. Isn't that the new coach of the Hundred Oaks baseball team and the new manager? (Truth sucks sometimes.)
4. Isn't that the new coach of the Hundred Oaks baseball team with some gorgeous model? (Ideal.)
5. Isn't that sweet Parker Shelton with some gorgeous male model? (Doubly ideal.)

So who knows how people interpreted my quitting the softball team? Sure, I was trying to prove I'm not like my mom, but did everyone realize that? Or did they think *Parker Shelton is a big ole quitter*?

And how is it fair to people like Brian, who tried so hard, for me not to even attempt playing again?

"I'll talk to Coach Lynn tomorrow," I whisper.

Brian chomps his gum as he stares out the window into the night. The moon and stars shine brightly on his smiling face. Then his smile fades. "I guess this means you won't be managing anymore."

"I guess not."

"I liked hanging out with you. It was fun. You're easy to talk to."

I bite back my grin. "I feel the same way."

"So I'll see you around?" he asks quietly. He turns to face me and drops a hand on my shoulder. His touch zaps my senses, and a jolt runs up my arm and down through my body to my toes and between my legs. Sin lightning. Or something.

I steal a breath. "I hope so."

"Me too." He folds his hands and glances up at my face.

"Thanks again. For everything," I say, and he nods before I climb out of his truck. I walk to the door and turn to wave bye. He waves back. The Ford's headlights flicker on as he reverses out of my driveway. I smell my arm, to see if I picked up his scent. Nothing.

The door pops open behind me, letting out lamplight and warm air.

"There you are," Ryan says. He peers over my shoulder at the driveway. I slip past my brother to go make dinner for him and Dad, who's stretched out on the couch watching a *Law and Order* rerun.

"Who was that?" Ryan asks, following me into the kitchen.

"It's nobody."

Nobody who I hope will become somebody very, very soon.

trust

I've had a chance to date before. Right before Mom left, before I quit the softball team, Jack Hulsey invited me to the Winter Wonderland formal. Jack was a senior and played center on the basketball team. The moment after he asked, a bazillion things ran through my mind.

Why would he want to take a girl like me? I'm overweight.

What color dress should I wear?

Should I make a hair appointment?

Get my nails done?

Will we go to dinner first?

Will I get my first real kiss at the end of the night? Or will he kiss me in front of everyone on the dance floor, when I'm curled up in his arms, swaying slowly?

Laura likes him. Laura likes him a lot.

Jack smiled while waiting for my answer.

I ended up going with Laura and Allie, and we giggled and danced and had a great time, but tears filled my eyes when I saw Jack slow dancing with another girl, kissing her.

It was okay, I decided. Laura would've made me feel guilty for accepting. Besides, I always put my friendships first.

Funny how Laura didn't return the gesture when I needed her more than anything. Are you there for me, God? Are you putting me first? Or is something else way more important in your eyes?

Written at the breakfast table on February 16. Burned.

• • •

Call me presumptuous, but I bring my cleats and workout clothes to school. I don't have any softball pants or jerseys that fit this 110-pound frame. I'll have to buy new stuff.

I blow out air before knocking on Coach Lynn's office.

"Come in," she says.

I open the door and step inside, and she beams.

"I can't wait to tell Coach Burns I'm stealing you," she says with a smile, touching her swollen stomach.

Late that afternoon, I accompany her out to the field, and when my cleats sink into the clay I suck on my bottom lip to stop myself from grinning like a crazy person. I gaze up at the lights, which are already blazing because the sun is beginning to set. The boys have just finished up their practice, and I wave at Drew, who gives me a thumbs up.

"Noooo, Parker, don't leave us!" Corndog yells, getting down on his knees and clasping his hands like he's praying. "I need you! Who's going to take care of my cup?"

I flip him the bird down low, making him laugh. Then a bunch of the guys get down on their knees and start begging me to come back to them, and I'm laughing and playing with my tangly ponytail, to calm my nerves.

Brian swings his bat in circles, raising his eyebrows, glancing from the boys to me.

The softball team has already gathered by the dugout. They're watching the baseball boys act like idiots, and envy flickers on their faces. A volcano erupts in Laura's eyes.

"Before we talk to the team," Coach Lynn says, "do you want to tell me why you quit in the first place?"

"Well, um, it was family problems and some issues with friends…" I feel my face burning up.

"I figure it must've been pretty serious."

"It was."

Coach Lynn nods and touches my shoulder. She leaves it at that, and I'm grateful. But it turns out she doesn't even need to tell the team. The minute I look at Laura, she lets out this whimper-scream-yelp thing that sounds like a puppy caught in a trap.

"Coach! No way!" Laura says, shaking her head like crazy.

Coach Lynn ignores Laura and looks from girl to girl. Some of them I know. Some of them I don't. Some of them I used to share clothes and Animal Crackers with.

"Parker Shelton's decided she wants to join the team this season. We'll see how she does in practice tonight and go from there in terms of choosing her position and where she'll bat in the lineup. But I imagine we'll try to put her at third."

"But, Coach, this isn't fair!" Laura whines. "We've been working out all winter, and practices have already started, and she just gets to waltz in and take over third base?" My former best friend looks like she might cry. Allie pats Laura's back and nods vehemently at the coach.

"It is fair," Coach Lynn replies, checking her watch. "I'm the coach, I make the decisions, and as captain, I hope you'll welcome Parker back, Laura."

Laura pounds her fist into her glove and bites her lip. I bet she's thinking: *if Parker rejoins the team, I won't be the best player anymore, and I have to be the center of everything or I'll just die.*

Some of the girls look at Laura with sympathy, but I notice a few girls rolling their eyes. I sort of want to tell them to stop, because our friendship was once good, and deep down, I still care about her.

Freshman year, one of our favorite things to do was to go tanning in her backyard. Then one day her dad, Brother John, decided to plant an apple tree right in the middle of our spot. Fourth of July was coming up, and Laura's older brothers had been stockpiling fireworks. We stole some in an attempt to blow up the apple tree, so we could have our tanning spot back.

Let's just say it didn't work. Her parents were pissed, but we laughed like maniacs, then rode our bikes to Dairy Queen for Blizzards, singing Taylor Swift songs at the top of our lungs.

"Pair off and start warming up," Coach Lynn says.

I pull my glove out of my bag and slip my hand into it. It feels soft, yet stiff, and it still smells like leather and dirt. Love. I pound my fist into it and chew my gum and whirl my arm around in a circle. My muscles ache, thanks to batting last night.

Everyone pairs off. I look from girl to girl, then one player—a sophomore whose name I can't remember—shrugs and approaches me.

"What's your name?" I ask.

"Sydney. I play catcher."

"I'm Parker. Wanna partner up?"

"Sure."

I nod and toss the ball at her, then take a step back. We keep stepping back until we're at least fifty feet apart. I don't miss a single throw.

"You've still got your arm," Coach Lynn says. "But you need to put some muscle back on."

I glance down at my body. The minute I start working out, I won't weigh 110 pounds anymore. Will any of my clothes fit? Will Laura call me butch again? A memory of leaving the locker room alone and crying flashes in my mind.

When it's time for batting practice, Coach Lynn instructs me to go first. The sun has completely set now, and the area beyond the field is black. I grab my favorite aluminum bat from my bat bag and jog up to home plate. I slip on a batting helmet and glance at Brian's truck.

His headlights come on, and he drives out of the parking lot. I wish he had stayed to watch me. Because, if I'm being honest with myself, he's a lot of the reason I'm doing this.

"Run on your fifth hit," Coach Lynn calls out. This means I'm supposed to hit the ball four times before running to first base after my fifth hit. I spread my legs apart and take a practice swing.

Laura winds up to pitch and whirls her arm around. The ball comes straight at my head. I fall to the clay, narrowly avoiding getting whacked. On the ground, I pant hard. On the mound, Laura cackles and digs her cleats into the mound. I lift my head to find Mel and Allie laughing, along with some other girls.

I lie back down on the ground, inhaling clay. This was stupid. Why did I think I could rejoin the team and everything would be okay? Because Brian, a twenty-three-year-old hot guy who knows nothing of my life, thought it would be a good idea? Well, it's not. Tears spring to my eyes, and my heart races.

"Laura!" I hear Coach Lynn yell. "Come on."

This was stupid, this was stupid. Stupid, stupid me.

"Parker?" I peek up. Corndog threads his fingers through the fence. I rest my forehead on the red clay.

"I'll bench you if you keep pulling this crap, Laura," Coach Lynn says. But I know she's lying. Laura's one of the best pitchers in our region. She could steal the principal's prized BMW and go mudding in it and the school would still let her play.

I feel hands gently lifting my arms. "You hurt?" Corndog asks quietly.

My pride is broken. I shake my head. "What are you doing here?"

"Lawnmower broke down."

I laugh softly. "Really?"

"Nah. Just wanted to see you bat. Then I was gonna take off." He helps me to my feet. I wipe dirt off my sweatpants. "Come on," he adds, leading me over to the dugout.

"You okay, Parker?" Coach Lynn calls, looking concerned.

"She needs a breather," Corndog replies. We sit down on the bench together, and I pull my batting helmet off and drop it on the patchy dirt floor. It bounces away.

"What happened?" he asks.

"Laura."

"I saw. But why let it bother you so much?"

I lift a shoulder and peek over at Corndog. A tear slips out of my eye and runs down my cheek.

"You're stronger than this."

"Why are you being so nice to me all of a sudden?" I ask.

"Competition's over. You won." He grins and laughs, looking out at the field. "Hey, listen," he says in a slow drawl. "I think it's cool you're going out for the team again. I never understood why you quit."

I drop my chin to my chest. I was right. Anyone can interpret my intentions however they want. "You think I'm a quitter."

"No...I just didn't get it. I could tell how much you loved the game."

"Oh really?" I glance at him.

"Remember sophomore year, during the Prom Decisional, how you stole third base and slid into me?"

"Yeah?"

"Your cleats dug into my shin and you knocked me down. And then you stretched out a hand and pulled me to my feet."

"Sorry about that..."

Corndog waves a hand. "I liked that you didn't gloat. You were just happy and playing the game."

"I love this game," I admit, watching as Laura steps up to the mound, whirls her arm, and pitches a strike right down the center. "But I don't trust this team."

Corndog looks confused and clutches his knees. "You gotta trust your team. I trust every single one of my guys."

I nod slowly, smiling a pained smile.

"You gonna go back out there now? You can do this."

I know I can do this. But do I want to? No, not really.

"Can you give me a ride home?" I ask him. Drew's long gone, and I don't feel like riding my bike tonight.

"As long as you don't mind riding my lawnmower. Left my truck at home."

I give him a tiny grin. "I'm up for an adventure."

● ● ●

Drew is one of those people everybody likes.

Even crazy Max Reddick, the guy who spends all his time carving sculptures out of Ivory soap, rushes to get a seat at Drew's art table.

On the first day of sixth grade, everyone was terrified of not knowing where to sit in the lunchroom. Students had graduated from three different elementary schools to attend Green Hills; middle school was another world. I felt lucky to know Laura, Allie, and Drew.

Will Whitfield had been homeschooled, so this was his first time learning with other kids. After paying for his lunch, he carried his tray in one arm and pushed his glasses up on his nose with the other hand. I saw the whole thing happen in slowmo. Someone jostled Will. The tray tilted.

The corndog went flying.

It hit JJ in the chest. JJ was, and still is, this huge football player, and he stood up and strutted toward skinny little Will. No one hits JJ with a corndog, that's for sure. I don't think JJ would've punched him or anything, but nobody wants to be humiliated on their first day at school.

"You're right, man! These corndogs are crap!" Drew yelled, launching a corndog straight at JJ's face.

Everyone knew Will as Corndog after that. Everyone knew him as Drew's friend.

The day Laura told everyone I was probably just like my mom—a butch softball player who likes girls—Drew crawled into my bed and held me until I cried out every tear in my body. He held me all night long.

Even with everything that's happened to me, I have to thank you for letting me keep Drew.

Written on February 17; kissed and tucked away in my Bible.

• • •

I'm sitting on my bed, removing my Passion Peach nail polish and chatting with Drew over Skype, even though he's right down the street. I tell him what happened with Laura.

"She's a jealous bitch," Drew replies.

I tell him about Corndog giving me a ride home on the lawn-mower, which was surprisingly fun, but very, very cold and windy. Not to mention bumpy.

"Huh," Drew replies. Pauses. "So...did you talk to Coach Hoffman today?" he yell-whispers over the Internet.

"I didn't see him."

That's not technically true, but I don't want to let on how I feel about him. I've never had a real *real* boyfriend, and I've never felt the urge to have a real relationship, 'cause what if the guy ditches me like Mom ditched Dad? Like Mom ditched me and Ryan? Like Laura and the other girls at church ditched me? A relationship never felt worth the risk.

Today I saw Brian when I arrived at school. He smiled and winked at me. I know, right? Scandal! But Drew doesn't need to know he winked. It's my secret. I set my cotton ball and nail polish remover on my bedside table and pull my laptop closer.

"What are you doing?"

Drew must be able to hear me typing. "Just checking my mail," I lie, opening Brian's Facebook page. I move the cursor over the "Add as Friend" button. I take a deep breath, close my eyes and push click. Now I wait. For a minute, for a month, forever.

I retrieve my cotton ball and get back to work on my thumb-nail, listening to Drew talk about the op-ed he's submitting to the *Franklin Times*. Then an email alert pops up at the bottom of my screen. *Brian Hoffman has accepted your friend request.*

I kick my feet up and down on the mattress and squeal for like, ten seconds straight. Ryan pounds on the wall with his fist and tells me to control my estrogen.

Drew blurts, "What's going on? Tell me!"

"Let me call you back," I say, disconnecting. I immediately click on Brian's profile and scan his wall. He posts lots of status updates regarding baseball scores and sports news—especially about the Braves and Georgia Tech. He also links to articles about healthy living, and it looks like he's planning to run the Nashville half-marathon in April and is raising money in support of the American Heart Association.

I check his relationship status: Single.

I squeal again, and Ryan pounds on the wall again. I fluff my pillows behind me and get comfy. I garner the courage to send him an instant message over Facebook. I have something to talk to him about, so why not?

Hey, I type.

Brian Hoffman: Hey.

Parker Shelton: Can I be manager again?

Brian Hoffman: So you're quitting already?

Parker Shelton: You behave or I'm leaving!

Brian Hoffman: Where'd you go? LOL. Come back.

Parker Shelton: You have to behave.

Brian Hoffman: Funny, I was about to say the same thing to you.

The cursor blinks for a few seconds.

Brian Hoffman: Are you going to tell me what happened?

Parker Shelton: Nope.

Brian Hoffman: Why'd you quit the team last year?

As comfortable as I feel with him, I can't tell him about Mom. Considering his parents go to Forrest Sanctuary, who knows how

Brian feels about homosexuality. I'm not ready to take the risk to find out yet. I'm enjoying this too much. Maybe one day, if I trust Brian enough, I'll tell him everything.

Really, that's what it all comes down to.

Parker Shelton: I don't trust the team

Brian Hoffman: Wow.

I pick at my nail polish. Then I type.

Parker Shelton: What's the point in playing for a team you can't trust? Isn't that the whole point of a team? To be part of something? I mean, last night when we went to the batting cages, I felt like I belonged there.

Brian Hoffman: With me?

I want to type *Exactly*, but I don't.

Parker Shelton: Can I be a manager again? I like being around Drew.

(And you, Brian Hoffman. But I don't type that.)

Brian Hoffman: I can't say I'm that disappointed you're not playing.

Yeah? I reply, and kick my feet up and down silently.

Brian Hoffman: Yeah, I need a good manager.

Parker Shelton: Oh, is that it?

Brian Hoffman: Good managers are hard to find. Filling coolers with ice is serious business.

Parker Shelton: Jerk.

Brian Hoffman: :) I wish you'd play, because you've got talent. But—

Parker Shelton: But?

Brian Hoffman: I'm glad you'll be around. I like talking to you. You're hilarious.

One thing's for sure: I get to spend a whole hell of a lot more time with Brian, and I can't wait.

• • •

The rest of the week is sucky *and* wonderful.

Sucky because, during lunch, I had to listen to Laura and Allie going on and on about how I'm nothing but a quitter.

Sucky because I never talk to Brian one-on-one in person. During gym, he stands with Coach Burns while the boys play basketball or volleyball, and I usually run past him when we girls are doing laps. I wear the shortest shorts I own and try to look as sexy as possible, even when doing sit-ups. He barely looks my way! But then at night, we message on Facebook. That's the wonderful part.

He has a dog, a black lab named Brandy. They go running together every morning before work. His favorite vacation spot is Destin, Florida—he loves the white sand beaches. After surviving an outbreak in fourth grade, lice scare him to death, and that's why he'd never consider teaching at an elementary school. His arch nemesis at school is Ms. Bonner, the home ec teacher, because she's always nagging him about his wrinkled shirts and slacks.

I told Brian she wants to iron his clothes as a prelude to a scandalous affair. He told me I have wicked, disgusting thoughts.

He knows I adore animals but that my biggest fear is granddaddy long-legs because once when I was little girl, a spider crawled into my glass of water in the middle of the night and I almost drank him. Brian knows I don't eat much—he's been scoping me out in the cafeteria, and he got on to me. He knows my favorite drink is the ninety-nine-cent fat-free latte from that janky machine down at the Highway 41 Exxon station. He knows I want to meet Brandy the black lab. Brian has black hair, so I asked if he and Brandy look alike, since dogs and owners are supposed to resemble each other. That made him *LOL*. I could see his smile over the Internet.

I keep painting my nails Passion Peach.

the first baseball game
44 days until i turn 18

On Saturday, the team meets in the parking lot to drive to Tullahoma for the first official game of the season. Drew and Sam are sipping water and gargling "Bad Romance." When they finish the song, Drew spits his water out on the pavement and says, "Any requests?"

Jackson Powers says, "Do 'Like a G6.'"

Drew laughs. "I can't rap! I'm a white hick last time I checked."

"Which explains why you do Lady Gaga so well?" I tease.

Drew hugs me from behind and musses my hair.

Corndog parks his truck in the lot and heads over, carrying his bat bag. His hair is all disheveled like he just rolled out of bed. It's kinda yummy looking. But not as yummy looking as Brian's—his is still wet. Like he got out of the shower and came straight here.

Corndog joins Drew, Sam, and me. "Glad you made it on time, Parker."

"Why wouldn't I?" I retort.

"Figured you were out late hooking up with somebody. Isn't that what you do on Fridays?"

I suck in a deep breath. Asshole.

"Come on, man," Drew says to him. "It's not her fault."

What's not my fault?

Corndog runs a hand through his hair. He has bags under his eyes. "Sorry…I had a rough night. Didn't mean to take it out on you."

"Whatever," I reply, bowing my head and moving a few steps away. I thought he and I were getting past this whole feud. Guess not. Guess I can't completely abandon my rep.

Brian appears beside me. "What's wrong?"

"I've been picking at my pinky nail all morning." I show him how I peeled some of the paint off.

"Aw, poor baby. Get on the bus." He grins mischievously, patting my back with his clipboard.

Okay, so riding on the boys' bus is like going to another planet. The moment I get onboard, the stench of dirty feet, sweat, and farting hits me in the face. On top of that, someone shoots a jockstrap like a rubber band and it nearly hits me in the face. I duck just in time.

"Knock it off, you assholes," Corndog says, flopping down in back with Drew and Sam. That's where the softball captain sits too.

"The only jockstrap Parker wants belongs to me," Paul says.

A smattering of laughter breaks out, and I blush, clutching the strap of my bag.

"Shut it, Paul," Corndog says, giving him a dirty look. "Take a seat," he tells me.

"I don't know where to sit," I reply. "Seniority and all."

"You'd better stay up front."

"Fine with me," I mutter when I realize I'll be right across the aisle from Brian, who's already immersed in the lineup, murmuring to himself. It's like he's having a love affair with his clipboard. Before we leave, he shuts his eyes for a long moment, then stands to face the team.

"Where's Coach Burns?" Corndog calls out.

"Corndog's got a hard-on for Coach!" someone yells. "Hot!"

"Stop being morons," Brian says, "And shut up and listen to me for a sec, okay?"

The guys actually do shut up. It's cool he's got their respect.

"Coach Lynn was sent to the hospital yesterday due to pregnancy complications," Brian says, and I gasp. I bite my tongue.

"And?" Corndog asks. "Is she okay? Is the baby okay?"

I peek around the edge of my seat to see him standing up at the back of the bus. He looks worried.

"I think she and the baby are fine," Brian says. "But the doctor says she has to go on bed rest for the remainder of her pregnancy. So Dr. Salter asked me to take over the baseball team while Coach Burns coaches softball this season. He has more experience with softball than I do." Brian swallows hard.

Oh. My. God. That means no supervision. Coach Burns won't be around to yell at Brian and me to stop chatting. I can't help but grin, even though I'm worried for Coach Lynn. She's a nice lady.

Brian's eyes shift to mine, then he goes back to talking to the team. "I know y'all love Coach Burns, but I hope I can fill his shoes, at least somewhat."

"I want to have *your* babies, Coach Hoffman!" Sam calls, cracking up the guys. Sam says that to pretty much everybody these days, so if he was being truthful, he'd have like eleven billion kids by now.

"Sit down, Henry," Brian says, and looks at the ceiling, as if praying for help. He turns to the bus driver. "Can we go already?"

The ignition cranks to a start, and then we're hurtling down the highway toward Tullahoma, passing farms and rolling hills. It's a beautiful, sunny February day. Too bad Corndog ruined the sun by being a jerk. I pull the new *Cosmo* out of my bag and start learning about these sit-ups that guarantee a six-pack in less than a month. I have a romance novel about cowboys in my bag that I'm dying to break out, but I don't want anyone to see it and make fun of me. It's called *The Lonesome Hero*, and the cover features a naked guy, a semi-naked girl, and a strategically placed horse trough.

Instead, I drown myself in an article about what kinds of bras are best for my body type until Corndog flops down next to me. He slouches and gazes over at me with tired eyes.

He blocks my view of Brian.

"What?" I mumble, shifting in my seat.

"I'm sorry about before. I'm stressed."

"Even if you're stressed, you can't be mean."

"Yeah, well, people don't expect a lot from you like they do me," he mutters, shutting his eyes.

"You don't know anything about me," I whisper. Stupid, stupid me, to let him take me home the other night. Stupid, stupid me to think I might be making a new friend. "Go away. Please."

"I came to apologize. I'm trying here."

"Maybe you should practice more."

He holds my gaze for a few seconds, his blue eyes piercing into me, and then he stands and disappears to the back of the bus.

I slide down in my seat, trying to control my breathing. I rip a page out of *Cosmo* and write:

Why is it, the minute everything begins to feel okay, you decide to test my faith again? Don't you get it? You won, God. You are the almighty and I'm just me, trying my best to live, to love.

Written February 20; thrown out the bus window.

• • •

"Parker."

I glance up from picking at a hole in my jeans. Brian wants me. "Yeah?"

"C'mere for a sec." He pats the bus bench. "I need to go over a few stats with you."

My hands tremble. I stand and see what the players are up to.

"Tell us how far you've gotten with her, man!" Paul asks Sam. They're talking about Jordan.

"Hell, no. I can't tell you. She'd rip my balls off," Sam replies, pounding a fist into his glove.

"She would totally rip his balls off," Corndog says, cringing.

None of them seem to notice me moving to slip into the seat with the coach. Our elbows touch but he doesn't pull away.

"What do you want to talk about?" I ask.

He turns the pages until he reaches a blank section for notes, then draws a Tic-Tac-Toe board. He pulls a pencil from behind his ear and hands it to me. I fill the center box with an *X*.

"This game is so stupid," I mumble.

He draws an *O*. "I know."

"Then why are we playing it?"

"You looked like you need to talk."

I jot down an *X*. "I don't feel like it."

"Then just sit here with me, okay?"

I shift a little, so our hips are touching too. Brian glances around, at the bus driver and over his shoulder.

"Want to play MASH instead?"

"What's that?" he replies.

"I used to play it in elementary school." I take the book and pencil and start writing down numbers from one to four. "It's this game where we figure out what kind of house and car you'll have, who you'll marry and stuff like that."

He groans. "Sounds girly."

I ignore him. "MASH stands for mansion, apartment, shack and house, but I like to play this my own way. Name four kinds of places to live. You know, a trailer or a Victorian-style house or whatever."

He ticks choices off on his fingers. "Log cabin, beach house, country farmhouse, and igloo."

I write down his choices. "Name four cars."

"Can they be other methods of transportation? Do I have to say lame things like Toyota Corolla and Ford Escort?"

I laugh. "You can say whatever method of transportation you want."

"Horse, Harley, submarine, and bicycle."

"I love riding my bike," I reply.

"I know. I see you riding all over the place."

"You stalking me?"

"Only on Wednesdays."

I give him an evil eye. "Name four women."

"Mila Kunis, Megan Fox, Lindsay Lohan, and Kim Kardashian."

I make a gagging noise.

Laughing, he looks over my shoulder at MASH as I jot down his answers. "Give me four places you want to go on your honeymoon."

"What honeymoon? I'm not getting married."

Yay! "A hypothetical honeymoon. Honestly, have you never played MASH before?"

"Nope."

"Amateur hour."

He grins and rubs the scruff on his jaw. "You're funny, you know that?"

"Stop sucking up and give me four places for your hypothetical honeymoon."

"Fine." He pauses to think. "Tokyo, Canberra, Venice, and Alaska."

I tell Brian about how I love picking up worn travel books at yard sales and paging through them in bed at night. My favorite guide is for Italy. Dad wants to visit there so bad.

"I've always wanted to travel," Brian says. "I've never left the States."

"Me neither. But I want to." I love that we have that in common. "Why haven't you?"

Lines appear on his forehead. "Haven't gotten around to it yet, I guess."

I begin drawing a pinwheel. "Tell me when to stop drawing."

"Stop," Brian replies. "What the hell is this game anyway?"

"Watch." The pinwheel has eight lines, so I begin going through his answers and cutting them out until I'm down to one of each.

"Okay, so you're going to marry Kim Kardashian and you'll go to Tokyo for your honeymoon. Then you'll live in a house at the beach and drive a submarine around."

He grins and chews his gum. He nudges me gently and glances over his shoulder for a third time. "You'd better go back to your seat now that you've predicted my future."

"Yes, sir," I mock, and slip across the aisle, grinning.

When God created the Earth, he had such a sick wicked sense of humor. He made everything that's wrong feel really, really good.

• • •

Before the game against Tullahoma starts, both teams stand on the sidelines as a girl sings the National Anthem.

The last ball game I went to was sophomore year. Mom watched me play, then we went out for smoothies and she kissed my cheek and told me how great I am at ball. Leaning against the dugout fence, smelling the clay and clipped grass and feeling the sunshine on my face reminds me of her. Her, her, her.

I breathe in and out, getting myself into the groove. I can do this. I want to be here. I say "Ommmm. Ommmm," under my breath, because *Cosmo* says that helps center your core.

"Parker," Brian calls out. "C'mere."

I jog to the other side of the dugout.

"What were you doing over there?" he asks.

"I was Ommm-ing. You know, centering my core?"

"Okay, Obi-Wan, take this lineup to the press box." He waves a scorecard.

"Can I have some gum, please?" I hold out a hand and he digs a package out of the back pocket of his gray baseball pants. He hands me a piece, shaking his head. I also take the list from his fingers and make my way across the field to the box. Guys on the other team start catcalling at me.

"You can play with my balls anytime you want, babe!" the other team's catcher yells, getting lots of laughs.

"Don't grip my bat too hard!" another one says.

Drew and Sam appear on either side of me, to walk me to the press box. The Wildcat players blow kisses my way. Drew jumps up and down and pretends to bat the kisses away before they reach me, making me smile.

Sam throws an arm around me. "Of all the sexist humor out there, they immediately jump to bats and balls? Lame."

I laugh softly. Now this is a team I can trust. Well, besides Corndog. He's a total flip-flopper.

We're up to bat first, so Sam puts his batting gloves on, grabs his bat and helmet, and heads toward home to lead off. I sit Indian style on the bench with the stats book on my lap and the pencil in my mouth, ready to go.

By the fourth inning, we're tied at two runs apiece. Paul hit a double that drove in Travis Lake and Drew hit a single to bring John Thames home.

Brian's standing on the dugout steps, leaning on one knee, fully immersed in the game.

"Coach," I whisper.

"You can't have any gum." He laughs to himself.

"I need to use the bathroom."

"Oh, Lord. Go. Hurry." He waves me away. "Wait. Give the stats book to Luke over there." He nods at a wiry freshman.

I dart out of the dugout and up the hill toward the concession stand and zip into the bathroom. The smell of popcorn and nachos wafting through the vents just about kills me.

I'm coming back from the bathroom when a little boy rushes past me, chasing a baseball. He slips and falls to the asphalt. I rush up and squat as he cries out and clutches his knee. Big tears fill his blue eyes. They're really pretty. Familiar.

"Hi," I say calmly. "Are you okay?"

He shakes his head. The tears drip down his cheeks, and he squeals.

"What's your name?" I ask softly, checking out the scrapes on his knees and palms.

He wipes his eyes. "Bo."

"That's a cool name. You like baseball, Bo?"

He nods.

"How old are you?"

He hiccups and lets out a sob, then holds up four fingers.

"Wow, you're big, huh?"

He nods again and clutches at his knee, where the skin is raw.

"Are your parents here with you at the game?" I ask.

He nods. All he does is nod.

"Can I pick you up and help you find your mom?"

Bo gasps and begins to shake all over. It's freaking me out. Is he having a seizure? I jerk my head around, searching for his parents.

"Don't worry," I tell him. "I like baseball too, and I know you want to watch the game with your parents, right?"

His head bobs up and down.

"Can I pick you up?"

"Okay," he whispers.

I lift Bo in my arms, and I'm moving toward the stands when Corndog sprints up and takes the little boy into his arms. "It's okay, it's okay," he whispers, kissing Bo's temple and patting his floppy brown hair. "Shhh."

"Is this your…?"

"Little brother. Did you get lost, buddy?"

Bo nods and hiccups again.

"Let's get you back to Daddy, okay?" Corndog says, hugging him.

"Nice to meet you, Bo," I say, starting to turn.

"What's you?" he replies.

"I think he wants to know your name," Corndog says, giving me a weird look.

"Parker. Have fun at the baseball game, okay?" I hustle back to the dugout before Brian gets all up in my grill for being gone so long.

"Can I have more gum?" I ask Brian, putting out a hand. He gives me another piece, and smiles before focusing on the game again. I retrieve the stats book and grab a seat on the bench. A minute later,

Corndog sits down and narrows his eyes and stares at me for a long time, like he's trying to figure something out.

"What?" I ask, slipping the new gum into my mouth.

"That was nice." He jerks his head toward the spot where I helped Bo.

"He was real sweet. His blue eyes are so pretty. Just like yours."

Corndog looks like he can't help but smile. "How'd you do that?"

I chew. "Do what?"

"How did you calm Bo down?"

"We talked. I dunno," I say with a shrug. We're in the middle of the lineup—I circle Drew's name in the stats book.

Corndog seems amazed. He grins again. "I'm surprised he talked to you. He's sorta, um, autistic," he whispers, his eyes darting around. "Bo's got Asperger's."

Having a sick brother must be tough. "Oh. Well, I couldn't tell anything's wrong with him."

He squeezes my wrist and searches my face, looking deeper than anyone has in a while. It gives me chills.

"It's really hard sometimes," Corndog says quietly. "Last night I heard my mom crying, and I got upset. That's why I was a dick today. I'm sorry."

"It's fine. Shitty stuff happens, you know?"

"I do know." He averts his eyes.

"Parker," Brian says, beckoning me. "Let's talk."

I walk over to Brian, carrying the stats book. "Yeah, Coach?"

"Stand with me, okay?"

"You double-checking my work?" I joke.

He chomps his gum. "I guess you could say that."

I'm smiling the rest of the game.

And we win four-two.

I'm very happy.

• • •

Now I'm very unhappy.

As the team's boarding the bus after the game, I'm watching Brian flirt with a woman who's with the Tullahoma softball team. Is she their coach? She's wearing a Wildcats parka, jeans, and ballet flats. Seriously? I can't believe he'd talk to a coach who'd dare to wear something so ridiculous onto a baseball field.

Then I look down at my clothes. Tight sweater, skinny jeans and Converses. My makeup is perfect, and I woke up extra early to tangle my hair. I guess I'm not behaving any better than Coach Vixen over there.

She's much prettier and curvier than me, and I can tell Brian likes her because he's leaning toward her and laughing at everything she says.

I should stop watching, but I can't look away. My chest hurts. My eyes burn. Then it gets worse: she pulls her phone out of her back pocket and hands it to him. He enters his numbers for her.

And to think I played MASH with him.

I stomp up the stairs to the bus and flop onto my bench. When Brian climbs aboard, I fold my arms across my stomach.

Sam is loudly telling this story about how he saw a hot pink dildo laying on the concrete behind the cafeteria back at Hundred Oaks and all the guys are hollering and carrying on, trying to guess how it got there.

"I bet it belongs to Ms. McCanly," Jake Sanders says.

"I bet it was put there by aliens!" Corndog calls out.

"Oh God," Brian groans.

I sneak a peek at him. His eyes are shut and he looks exasperated, thanks to the tale of the dildo. He glances over at me and smiles. "C'mere."

I'm pissed, but I slide across the aisle anyway. None of the guys are paying attention to me. Dildos are way too distracting.

"What?" I ask, making sure not to touch him.

"What's wrong? You've been upset a lot today."

I pick at the hole in my jeans.

"Is this 'cause I'm marrying Kim Kardashian?"

A laugh escapes my lips. "No."

"Then what is it?" he asks softly. There's care in his voice.

I look out the window as we fly past cornfields. "Who was that lady you were talking to? You know, Coach Vixen in the ballet flats."

"Coach Vixen?" he exclaims. "Coach Black? Jenna?"

"Yeah, Coach Vixen."

He gives me a knowing smile. "Are you stalking me?"

"Only on Wednesdays."

He laughs, chewing his gum. "I went to high school with her. We haven't seen each other in years."

"She's pretty."

"She's all right," he replies, shaking his leg up and down.

I suck on my bottom lip.

He jabs me softly in the side. "Let's play another round of that MASH game of yours. I want to see if I can live in an igloo, drive a tractor, and marry Angelina Jolie instead."

sinner extraordinaire

43 days until i turn 18

On Sunday, Dad, Ryan, and I head to church. This morning I had to pound on Ryan's door for five minutes before he woke up. Sweat drenched his clothes, and he could barely open his eyes as he rubbed his face. He leaned against the wall before making his way to the shower. I made him scrambled eggs and toast to fill his stomach and hopefully clean out whatever he drank/ate/snorted/shot up last night.

When I confronted Dad in the laundry room about Ryan, he said, "Your brother's an adult." He moved wet socks from the washer to the dryer. "I can't tell him how to live his life." Then Dad put an arm around my shoulder, kissed my head, and told me to call Mom sometime.

Daddy Denial, as always. I find it funny that Dad makes Ryan come to church, which seems to be telling him how to live his life, if you ask me.

The Durango pulls into the parking lot, and I see Tate standing by himself by the swing set. I hop out of the car and skip over to him.

"Doughnuts?" I ask.

Tate laughs. "You've been hungry lately."

"I'm famished," I reply, looking down at his tie that's covered by music notes. His hair is all crazy gelled up, but I like it. Together we start walking to the Fellowship Hall. He fumbles with something in his pocket.

"Where's Aaron?" I say.

"Uh, he went inside already," Tate replies.

"Why?"

"You, um, never returned his calls…"

"So…?" I look at Tate sideways.

"So he thought you were interested."

"I never said anything, though," I blurt.

"But you made out with him. What's he supposed to think?"

Leave it to Tate to give it to me straight. Because he went to other schools, I never really knew him until after Mom left. That's when he started hanging around.

"So what, Aaron and I can't be friends?" I ask, playing with my hair.

Tate lifts a shoulder. "I dunno, you should talk to him."

Inside the church, Tate and I get in line for Coffee Time, and that's when I see Aaron and Laura across the Fellowship Hall. Laughing and smiling and touching each other.

"Are you kidding me?" I mutter, nudging Tate and pointing. Laura just fed Aaron a grape! In Sunday school last week, she started crying because she was worried people she knows are going to Hell. She looked at me pointedly. But it's okay for her to flirt at church?

"Is he actually interested in her? If so, why?"

Tate scratches his neck. "I dunno. She answers when he calls. Why? Do you care?"

"Not really." Truth. Last night, I could've gone to Miller's Hollow and hung out with somebody, but I stayed in and chatted with Brian over Skype. And that connection felt better than kissing could ever feel.

That's when I see him. Standing across the room drinking coffee from a Styrofoam cup. Brian raises his eyebrows at me, and I can see him smiling behind the cup. He's wearing his Best Buy costume: white shirt, black tie. So nerdy hot.

I peer around the room. Ryan's sitting between a piano and a potted plant with his head up against a wall. Dad is deep in conversation. With a woman! She looks like she might be from India. She's gorgeous, with long black wavy hair and a nice smile. Jack Taylor of the Jack Taylor Ford dealership looks at them like they have the plague. Dad's so busy talking to Mystery Woman he doesn't even notice Jack. Or me.

I touch my stomach. "I need to use the bathroom. Damned stale doughnuts."

Tate laughs. "TMI."

I toss my napkin and cup in the trash and head toward the bathroom down the hall. Fifteen seconds later, Brian appears. We smile but don't say a word. He glances over his shoulder. I lead him past the women's restroom to the janitor's closet. Inside, it's dark. I pull on the chain cord that turns on the light and glance around at the bottles of Windex and Clorox. The stench of bleach nearly knocks me down. I'm panting.

I climb the ladder that leads up to a crawl space above the supplies. I tell Brian I know about this place because Laura and I would hide here sometimes as kids, during church-wide games of Hide and Seek. The cubby has very little space—the last time I was up here I was nine—so he and I are touching elbows and legs when we squeeze in.

"Hi," he says, grinning.

"Hi…Do you have a second job at Best Buy?"

"What? No." He looks down at his clothes and realization dawns on his face. "You smart ass. Trouble." His mouth twitches in amusement. "I bet there are lots of spiders up here."

I smack his bicep. "Shut up, you."

He shoves me with his elbow.

I smile at his lips. "You came to church."

He plays with his bangs and looks at me sideways. "Yeah. I figure I need to repent for my sins."

My eyes go all buggy. I gasp. Is he thinking the same sinful things about me that I'm thinking about him?

"What sins?"

"When I was six, I stole a Three Musketeers bar from Walmart. When I was nine, I scribbled Evan's name on a desk with permanent marker and denied I did it. He had to scrub it off. In high school, I wrote the Pythagorean Theorem on my palm and cheated on a test."

"But other than that, you're perfect?"

"Totally perfect."

I want to touch his knee and run my hand up his thigh, but I keep my hands folded tight in my lap. He crosses his arms. We've talked every night this week. He knows that sometimes I wear a My Little Pony T-shirt to bed. I decide being up front is best.

"Do you consider me a sin?" I whisper, my hands fidgeting.

"Talking to you? No. But…anything else? Yes, that would be bad."

"Bad?" My voice shakes and squeaks.

He loosens his black tie. "Listen…I think you're beautiful, and really smart and funny and kind—"

My heart swells, my pulse races, my grin explodes.

"But I teach at your school. You're a minor." He gives me a sad smile.

Everything slows to a stop. I'm ready to cry. I mean, why would he come up here with me, if not to do something more? We've been talking every night on Skype and chat. What is that supposed to mean?

"We're friends, right?" he asks, taking my hand.

My face hurts from frowning so hard. Friends don't hide in janitors' closets to talk to each other.

He nudges me with his elbow. I lean against his shoulder, and he tells me about how, this morning, he ran fifteen miles in two hours, his best time yet. He's in perfect shape to run the Nashville half-marathon in April.

"Why are you raising money for the American Heart Association?"

He holds my gaze for several seconds before rubbing the back of his neck. "It's a good cause. My grandmother died of a heart aneurism."

I squeeze his hand. "I bet she was a great person."

"I loved her."

I can tell he wants to change the subject. "You know what's also a good cause? Buying me cheese fries at Foothills Diner." I wink at him.

"I knew I would convert you to the cult of Fries à la Appalachia. You should eat more of them. You need to put on weight."

"Naw, I like being skinny." He scans my body slowly, and when he looks up into my eyes, he jerks his neck, flipping hair off his forehead. He pulls his knees to his chest and clutches his shins.

I grab his wrist and pull it closer to check his watch. It's so dim in here. "We should go. Dad'll kill me if I miss Big Church."

"Big Church?" Brian says, chuckling.

"Don't ask."

I climb down the ladder, and Brian puts his hands around my waist and helps me to the floor. I turn around to face him and stare up at his chapped lips. Does he bite them? Is he stressed? He avoids my eyes and gestures toward the door. We exit the janitor's closet and

I run straight into Mystery Woman. She sees Brian emerging behind me. She throws us a questioning look, then goes into the bathroom.

"Damn," I whisper to him.

"Just keep walking," he whispers.

I hustle down the hallway and up the stairs to the sanctuary, but by the time I get there, Brian's not behind me anymore. He just…left?

I play zombie all through the service, acting like I'm in the sanctuary, but really I'm in that janitor's closet. Our arms touching. Sharing the same Clorox-infused air. My mind wanders when we sing my favorite hymn, "I'll Fly Away," because the words are beautiful, but when the organ goes silent I'm thinking of his chapped lips again.

After Big Church, everyone shakes hands and chats for a while before leaving. I avoid Aaron and Laura, who are looking at each other like they're getting married in an hour, but Tate asks where I disappeared to during Sunday school.

"The doughnut was way staler than usual," I lie.

Outside in the parking lot, I lean up against the Durango and wait for Dad. Will Brian want to talk later today? Is this it for us? Should I stop talking to him altogether? Should I settle for being friends? Can my heart handle only being friends? Could I bring up April fifth again to see if we could hang out after that? Could I bring up hanging out after graduation?

"I want you to meet my daughter."

I look up to find Dad standing there with Mystery Woman, smiling like someone just handed him a winning lottery ticket. I gasp and cross my arms and look around. I blush. She studies me like I'm a difficult calc problem.

Dad beams. "Parker, meet Veena. Veena, meet Parker."

• • •

When I was little, I looked up to Ryan. He was my hero: so good at baseball, so smart at school, so funny and cool with his friends. I felt like a twerp by comparison.

Opryland was Nashville's theme park, but it went out of business a couple of years ago. It had this crazy 3-D rollercoaster called Chaos. It scared the bejesus out of me. I loved the bumper cars. I ate cup after cup of Dippin' Dots ice cream. But my favorite attraction was the Tin Lizzie cars. Kids could drive horseless carriages from the early 1900s around a track. I did that over and over again. One time, when I was eight, I took off for the Tin Lizzies, thinking my family was right behind me.

They weren't.

I ran around in circles, crying. My parents told me never to talk to strangers, so I wouldn't let anyone who was trying to help me come near. I was lost for ten minutes before Ryan found me. I'll never forget how he came sprinting up and lifted me into his arms and twirled me in a circle. My running off scared him bad.

Now, I wish I had a Tin Lizzie that I could drive to find the real Ryan. The one I love and miss. Where did he run off to? And God, will you bring him back?

Written on February 21 on a napkin. Wadded up and burned.

• • •

I have never ever sat by the phone before. Never. Ever.

But that's how I'm spending Sunday afternoon, instead of my usual: doing homework. Ring, phone, ring! He has my number—I gave it to him over Skype. Hell, he can talk to me on Skype if he wants to. But he hasn't been online all day. The only thing in my inbox is a draft article Drew wrote that he wants an opinion on.

I compose a short email to Brian:

Hey, where did you disappear to today? Loved talking to you in the janitor's closet. It's my new favorite place. Let's do it again sometime. Next Sunday during Big Church?

Egads, what am I thinking? I delete the email immediately and pray that no hacker saw that and plans to post it all over the Internet announcing it as the lamest thing anybody's ever seen.

Maybe Brian's online but invisible. Maybe he's staring at my name and thinking, *Wow, she has no life and she's sitting there waiting for me to message her. I'm gonna go running with Brandy the dog and then go drink a beer and live my real adult life and do adult things.*

I click the Go Invisible button. Now he'll think I have a life. He'll think I'm out doing cool things, like hanging at Jiffy Burger with Drew, Corndog, and Sam, pretending to be Elaine and yelling "Get out!"

What if he's with Coach Vixen? What if they're doing it right now?

This goes on for two more hours. I download that movie *Never Been Kissed* starring Drew Barrymore from iTunes. As if anyone would actually believe a twenty-five-year-old woman who looks like her—hideous makeup or not—has never been kissed. Her teacher, who thinks she's a teenager when she's really twenty-five, is into her, but he doesn't go after it until he discovers she's really an adult.

I consider telling Brian that I'm not really a teenager. Really, I'm a twenty-five-year-old reporter for the *Tennessean* and I'm researching the athletics department at Hundred Oaks High because the football team gets all the money.

My phone buzzes. I pick it up faster than a jet at Mach 5. Aw, it's just a text from Corndog that reads Look outside ur window.

I move my laptop and go push the curtains aside to find Corndog sitting out front on his lawnmower. Without bothering to check my hair or makeup, I head to the front door. He gives me a big smile when I let him inside. He's wearing a polo layered on top of long-sleeved T-shirts with a pair of jeans, sneakers, and a cap.

Ryan's listening to some god-awful trance music in his room, and Dad is passed out on the couch with the Sunday comics draped across his face, so they don't even notice a boy coming in. That's what I should tell Brian. *I'm the real adult in my house, you know.*

Corndog follows me to my room without a word. As soon as the door's shut, I yell-whisper, "What are you doing here?"

He shrugs and rubs his palms together. "Bored. I don't have any homework or practice or chores so I thought I'd see what you're doing."

"Me?" We've never really hung out alone before, considering (1) he was my nemesis for valedictorian, and (2) he's never tried to hang out alone with me before. At least not since those science projects we did together in eighth grade.

His mouth slides into a smile. "Yes, you."

"Don't you need to do something on the farm?"

"Cows are milked. Eggs are collected. I got the afternoon off."

"How's Bo? Did he get booboos on his knees and hands?"

"Yeah. But he'll be okay."

Corndog starts looking around my room and beelines straight for my bookshelves. He drags a finger over my shelf o' vampire novels, then moves on to the travel guides I grab at yard sales and used bookstores. I love collecting random travel books for places like the Galapagos and Australia and Tanzania and South Africa.

Then he moves on to my nonfiction shelf, which has all sorts of randomness…books on zookeeping, books on the horrors of animal smuggling, books about the Serengeti. I'm praying he doesn't pull any of those books down, because I hide my Harlequin romances behind them.

Corndog starts looking at my bulletin boards, which are covered with pictures of me and Drew and me and my family. I took down the pictures of me, Laura, and Allie and buried them in a box under my bed. There's only one picture of me and Mom. It was taken when I was five, out in front of Forrest Sanctuary on Easter. Mom looked gorgeous that day in a trim blue dress and matching hat.

"What were you doing before I got here?" he asks, coughing into a fist.

Stalking your baseball coach online. "I was watching a movie."

"What movie?"

"This chick flick thing."

"My favorite!" he laughs.

"Corndog, why are you here?"

"I told you. I'm bored and wanted to hang out. Can't George hang out with Elaine once in a while?"

"I guess so."

He pulls his sneakers off, then lies down on my side of the bed—the side I sleep on!—and situates the laptop on his thighs. He yanks his cap off and tosses it on top of his sneakers. I hesitate for a sec, then lie down on the other side of the bed while he restarts the movie.

"I've never seen this," he murmurs.

We watch the movie in a nice silence until he exclaims, "This is unbelievable. How can they make Drew Barrymore look that bad? Well, I mean, she's still hot—I'd do her, but geez!"

I'm cracking up. "I know! And the teacher still wants her even though she's wearing that hideous sombrero."

"What a perv that guy is. What kind of teacher goes after his student?"

I clutch my pillow. "He probably has some sixth sense and knew that she wasn't really seventeen."

"A sixth sense."

"Yes."

"You think that perv guy has a sixth sense?"

"Yes. He has the ability to tell if women are really older than they say they are. He can tell when forty-year-olds are pretending to be thirty-five too."

He hoists himself up on an elbow and throws me a withering look. "Are you really our valedictorian?"

"Uh, yeah. I beat you by a tenth of a point, remember?" I chuckle. "Besides, we can't have someone named Corndog giving the vale-dictory speech. Everyone would spend the whole time salivating instead of listening. Everyone would just get up and leave to go get a corndog!"

He laughs, but then his face goes soft and pensive. "It's Will. You can call me that, you know."

"But no one would have any idea who I'm talking about."

A pause. "I kinda like that."

"You're talking over the movie," I say, gesturing at Drew Barrymore making an ass of herself singing with a band at a bar. She was stupid enough to eat a brownie full of roofies or something.

I snuggle up with Patrick the stuffed koala and Corndog? Will? slides a hand behind his head and we watch the movie together.

I guess at some point I passed out, because I wake up to find a black screen. I also find my mouth pressing against Corndog/Will/

Person/Guy's shoulder. I left a big drool spot on his polo. Holy mortifying! I'm pawing at it, trying to make my spit bleed into the shirt, when he opens his eyes and looks over at me with a lazy smile.

"Sorry, I drooled on you," I say.

"It's fine." He ruffles his hair. A cowlick sticks straight up. One eye opens wider than the other.

Oh. My. God. I fell asleep with a boy in my bed.

The sun is setting outside the window, leaving my room in shadow. It's nice lying here with him in a warm silence. It's pretty weird that he just dropped by and hasn't tried to make out with me or do any other funny business. I don't think this has happened before, well, at least not with anyone other than Drew. And he doesn't count.

So what's this about?

Will folds the laptop lid down and sets it on the floor, then shuts his eyes, pulls Patrick the koala to his chest, and curls up. I stare at the ceiling. How weird is this? The captain of the baseball team is cuddling with my stuffed animal? I shrug and shut my eyes and wonder if Brian's spending a quiet afternoon reading. I let myself doze back off.

Next thing I know, Dad has barged into my room. "I've been knocking for over a minute. What's going on in here?" he exclaims.

I sit up straight and smooth my tangles. Will quickly pulls himself to a sitting position, grabs his sneakers, and fumbles with the laces.

"Just watching a movie, Dad." I yawn.

"Who is this boy in your bed? And why's there a lawnmower by our front door?"

"This is Corndog," I say. "He's a friend from school."

Dad raises an eyebrow. "A friend?"

Why is Dad choosing this precise moment to stop being Daddy

Denial? *Gar.* It's not like I really care—I mean, this is just Corndog— what if Brian were in my bed?

"I better go," Corndog says, giving me a nervous smile.

"I'll walk you to the front door." I hop out of bed and lead him down the hall. When we get to the living room, I stop dead. Mystery Woman Veena is here. Staring at me. She looks from me to Corndog and back to me again.

Who is this lady? Some angel of darkness God sent to confront me for my sins? Thanks but no thanks, God. I've already got Laura.

Dad walks up behind me, whistling. He drops a hand on my shoulder. "I invited Veena over for dinner."

"I'll see you at school tomorrow," I mumble to Corndog. My face feels hotter than a supernova.

He glances at Dad and Veena, then gives me a quick smile. "Thanks for the chick flick."

Once he's gone, Dad claps his hands together and looks at me. "So what's for dinner?"

"Oh, um…" I say. I hadn't really thought about dinner yet. I glance at my watch. It's 6:00 p.m., and normally I've started cooking by now. Veena narrows her eyes at Dad. I guess he invited her over for dinner and failed to mention that his daughter makes most of the meals.

"I love cooking," I explain, not wanting to embarrass my father. "I accidentally fell asleep. I'll start making dinner now." I nervously play with my hair as I head into the kitchen. Pasta is a good, fast option. I don't have time to make a roast or anything. I could toss a salad to go with it. I grab a pot from the wall and begin filling it with water.

Brian hasn't called all day. Didn't that time in the closet mean anything to him? Obviously not.

I'm shutting off the water when Dad enters the kitchen. "Forget cooking. Let's go out for a change, okay?"

• • •

Ryan said he has a paper due tomorrow (can you say "excuse"?), so it's just me, Dad, and Mystery Woman Veena at Davy Crockett's Roadhouse. I like this place because they serve peanuts by the bucket, and I can eat a bucket load of peanuts because my diet depends on lots of protein.

I crack open a few and line eight peanuts up across my bread plate. I'll savor them one by one.

"Veena's a nurse," Dad says, touching her hand.

She blushes. Is she embarrassed of her job? Or because Dad is coming on way strong? Since when does Dad come on to anybody? He hasn't dated since…since…ever? Since Mom.

"I work at the Murfreesboro Regional Medical Center," she says, avoiding my eyes.

Dad rattles peanuts in his fist like a pair of dice. "And Parker is a senior at Hundred Oaks. She's going to Vanderbilt next year."

"Vanderbilt? Really?"

"She's valedictorian too," Dad adds, smiling and popping a peanut in his mouth.

I'm pleased that Dad is proud of me, but Veena looks way surprised. How humiliating. But then I remember: she doesn't know me. She has no right to judge me. Is that why she agreed to come out with us—to judge me? But on the other hand, all the evidence I've given as to my personality involves me hanging out with two different guys on the same day. One in a janitor's closet, one in my room. I rub my eyes. This isn't what I wanted for myself. Maybe I was meant to be a sinner. Maybe that's all I'll ever be. Maybe Laura's right.

A good person wouldn't lust after a teacher. Lonely or not.

Veena takes a greasy roll from the bread basket and butters it up. Saliva forms in my mouth as I stare at the bread. I could have one bite, right? No, I shouldn't.

"Are you coming to Forrest Sanctuary now?" I ask Veena.

She sips her water, then nods. "Yes. I just moved here from New York and don't really know anyone except for people at the hospital. But I've always gone to church, so here I am." She shrugs and blushes again. It gives her dark skin a rosy touch.

"I'm glad you came," Dad replies. He touches her hand again. "Excuse me, I'll be right back." He stands and heads toward the restrooms.

I eat the first of my eight peanuts, savoring the salt.

Veena takes a bite of roll, and after swallowing, she whispers, "Don't worry. I won't say anything to your father about this morning."

I find her eyes. They are kind but questioning.

She continues, "The man you were with…he seemed older."

I don't respond. I concentrate on peanut #2. I want to eat it in peace.

"It's none of my business, I know. And I'm one to talk…your father must be over ten years older than me…I'm 29…I just wanted to let you know I won't say anything, okay?" she says.

"Okay, thank you," I whisper. "Nothing happened, just so you know."

She pauses. "So, Vanderbilt?"

"Yes, I got in early admission." I say it with a strong, proud voice.

She smiles. "Good school. I didn't get into their medical program. I'm jealous."

"I studied hard."

"I guess I didn't study hard enough." She laughs, sipping her water, and I join in laughing.

I eat peanut number two and smile at Veena as I chew. She's very pretty and slim. I love her black curls, and it looks like she knows how to use an eyelash curler. Her full lips are painted a bronze-ish color.

Dad hustles up and slides into the booth next to her. "What did I miss?" he asks, putting his napkin back on his lap.

"None of your business," Veena replies. "Girl talk."

I pop peanut number three in my mouth and think: don't mess this up, Dad! She's pretty nice.

But she knows about Brian. I hope she keeps her mouth shut like she said she would.

• • •

Before bed, I wash my face with cleanser, moisturize, and carefully tweeze my eyebrows. I slip on pajamas and climb into bed with my laptop.

My phone beeps. A text from Corndog reads: Had fun today.

I text back: Me too. Can't wait to tell everybody u love chick flicks!

Don't! You'll destroy my street cred!

I log in to Skype, and ten seconds later an IM from Brian pops up.

Brian Hoffman: Hey. Sorry I flaked.

I smile, and a warm feeling rushes through my body.

Parker Shelton: No prob.

Brian Hoffman: Want to talk?

Parker Shelton: Yes!!

Skype rings, I answer, and Brian's voice tumbles out of the speakers. "Hey, you."

"Hi."

"Tell me about your day."

My phone buzzes again. I ignore it.

• • •

Drew and I don't have many classes together.

I'm taking AP courses, while he's in classes like music theory and art. It's senior year and he wanted to relax. But we do take AP English together, because he cares a lot about making his writing the best it can be. He sits in the front row, next to Corndog, and I sit right behind them. And because everyone now knows Drew broke up with Amy, the girls are out in full force to win his heart. Or win a chance to fool around with him. I don't know which.

While we're waiting on the final bell to ring before class starts, Marie Baird is leaning against his desk, chatting, laughing, and playfully slapping his shoulder, and Kristen Markum is standing between his legs, smiling down at him. He grins up at them, shaking his leg and tapping his foot. They're discussing what one item they'd bring if they were to go on the TV show *Survivor*.

"I'd bring my iPad so I could download books to read," Marie says.

"But how would you charge the battery on a deserted island?" I hear Corndog murmur to himself. I laugh silently.

"I'd bring a big pad of paper and pen so I could work on my autobiography," Drew tells them.

"I want to read it!" Kristen says.

"So do I," Marie adds.

"I'd bring a cell phone, so I could call you," Kristen says to Drew.

"But how would you charge the battery?" Corndog mutters to himself again, and I start laughing.

Corndog lobs a note onto my desk. I unfold the paper. *How does Drew always get this mad play?*

I write back: *Because he's Double-wide Drew.* I toss the note to Corndog; he catches it one-handed and reads. Then bursts out laughing. He writes me back.

Is that all girls care about? Penis size?

113

You better believe it. (Just kidding. We care about how much $$ you have too.)

Marie? Is that who he's interested in? Corndog writes.

No idea. She's pretty and nice, though.

Yeah, she's hot.

Why don't you just ask him?

I fold the note and move to toss it to Corndog, but Drew intercepts my pass. "What are you talking about?" He unfolds the paper and I swipe at him, trying to get it back, but he blocks me with a forearm. Ugh, he's such a football player. Corndog doesn't seem to care that our note has been hijacked, because he's giggling like a little girl.

Drew reads the paper. "Why are y'all writing notes about my junk?"

I bite my lips together to stop myself from laughing.

"I know you can't help but think about my package all day long," Drew says to me. "But English class is not the time or place to obsess over it." He snorggles and flicks my forehead. I flick his forehead. And then we're in a forehead flicking war.

"She's so boy crazy, it's pathetic," Kristen whispers to Marie, throwing me a glare. I suck in a deep breath. Corndog avoids my eyes and turns to face the whiteboard.

I sink down into my seat, embarrassed. My rep must be pretty bad if Kristen Markum, the girl who gets it on with everybody, thinks I get around.

• • •

Brian works us like plow horses in gym class.

But there is a bit of good news. I get lots of smiles from him as I run laps around the track.

I speed past Laura just in time to hear her comment on how cute Brian is, and how it's too bad he's our gym teacher. It's a good thing Brian's busy yelling at the baseball players in Coach Burns's class to pay any attention to her.

I'm on lap six of twelve, thinking about Brian's chapped lips and wondering why he bites them so hard, when Corndog jogs up next to me.

"Hey, Parker," he says, loping along, arms flailing all over the place.

"Your form sucks today," I reply.

"I'm tired. I stayed up too late texting."

I laugh. We have been texting a lot. Corndog and I talk about books and animals and how I might become a zookeeper and how he wants to study agricultural law one day. A lawyer for farmers?! I texted him last night.

A soil expert, he replied. One of the reasons farming has become so hard for people is soil erosion. It's become chemically altered because people overuse it.

Part of me wishes we could've been close friends before our last semester, but considering we spent three and a half years duking it out over grades, this is the first time we've been able to relax around each other.

"You stayed up late texting?" I tease. "That was very wrong of you. You should be removed as captain. You are a horrible influence on these young minds."

He laughs, his brown hair flopping in the wind. "You're the bad influence."

"Me?" I blurt.

"You're jogging with me. All the other girls want to be like you. They're gonna be all over me now." He jerks his head, indicating I should look behind us, and sure enough, Kate Kelly and Emily Mansfield are following, checking us out. Those girls are goody two-shoes who go to my church, and started ignoring me after Mom left. Everyone knows Kate's had a huge crush on Corndog for a century.

"I highly doubt anyone wants to be like me," I say, wiping sweat off my forehead.

"You slaughtered my GPA and ruined my lifelong dream of being valedictorian and—"

"Corndog!" Brian yells, waving his hand in a circle. "Pick up the pace."

"Coach, come on!" Corndog snaps, but he starts running faster than I could ever hope to run.

I go back to jogging by myself, and when I pass Brian, he narrows his eyes and mouths, "Corndog?"

I shake my head and give him a knowing smile. I feel a shift: Brian doesn't have all the power. Is he waiting on me to make a move?

insurance paperwork, monster burgers, and matching furniture

Saturday's game is at home.

We're playing Coffee County Central, one of the biggest schools in Middle Tennessee. They are damned good at baseball. Better than Hundred Oaks. Every year when we play them, we play for the Coffee Pot. It's a trophy in the shape of a coffee pot. It's stupid, really, but all these guys would go to war for that trophy. Anyhow, Brian is taking this game super seriously and keeps taking the stats book out of my hand, combing over the numbers, and handing it back.

And he doesn't mention last night's conversation at all. We chatted online for a few minutes before he went out with a high school friend. I prayed that "bowling with an old buddy" isn't code for "I'm having sex with Coach Vixen tonight."

Are you wearing a bowling shirt? I had asked.

Brian Hoffman: No. A button down. What are you wearing? :)

A bowling shirt, I lied.

Brian Hoffman: LOL

I garnered some guts and typed, I wish I could go bowling with you.

Brian Hoffman: Oh yeah?

Parker Shelton: I want to hang out with you. Alone. Together. You know?

Brian Hoffman: Like in the closet at church last week? :)

We could hang out in a nuclear reactor for all I care, I pressed Enter and pulled a deep breath.

The cursor blinked and blinked.

Brian Hoffman: You're fun. I wish we could hang out too...

He seemed wistful. Like it would never happen. But I also could tell I have a shot. A shot I desperately want.

I decided to play the hard-to-get card, I guess it'll never happen, eh?

Brian Hoffman: I don't know about never.

Parker Shelton: It's too bad it can't be sooner rather than never.

Brian Hoffman: I know, I know......I have to run.

Parker Shelton: Ok, see you tomorrow at the game.

Brian Hoffman: See you.

Right as I was about to sign off, Brian wrote, Soon. We'll hang out soon.

I did a bit of Internet sleuthing after our call. I looked up the age of consent for Tennessee. Not because I think Brian and I will have sex, but because I wanted to know how bad this is. My wanting him. Turns out the age of consent is 18, unless the partner is less than four years older.

That scared me, but nonetheless, now I find myself hoping that hanging out soon means today.

While most of the team is on the field during the top of the seventh inning, and we're losing four to one, Brian's leaning over onto his knee and yelling at Travis Lake to get into the game at shortstop.

I take a chance and tug on his jersey sleeve.

"What?" he asks, barely throwing me a glance.

"How was bowling?"

"Boring. It was just me and Evan."

"Evan is boring?"

"He's no Parker." He smiles slightly, then claps a couple of times and hollers to Jake Sanders that he's pitching a great inning. "Evan spent the whole time talking about how he hates changing his kid's diapers."

"That should be a lesson to you," I say, barely able to contain my laughter.

"Oh?"

"Maybe you should hang out with me while you've got the chance." I can't believe how bold I am toward him.

"Focus on stats, will you?" he says, chewing his gum and smiling.

We lose the Coffee Pot five to one. After storing the coolers in the equipment shed, I head back across the field toward the bike racks. The softball team is already warming up for their game.

"How old do you think he is?" Laura asks Allie, gazing over at Brian.

"Twenty-three," I say, skipping past. I can't help but smile, because I know the answers to everything they want to know.

"Parker," Brian calls, beckoning me with two fingers. I can feel Laura's eyes burning holes in me.

I hustle up to him, summoning my cutest smile. He adjusts his cap and chomps on his gum. "Have any plans this afternoon?" he asks quietly.

"Nope."

"You know the park by Little Duck River?"

I nod.

"I'll be there with Brandy at about four o'clock. She likes the water."

"That river has water moccasins! You shouldn't let Brandy play in there."

"Aw, come on. My dog ain't afraid of no snake. Snakes are scared of my dog."

"Oh, is that it?" I laugh.

From beside his truck, Corndog calls out from across the parking lot, "You need a ride home, Parker?" He jingles his keys.

"I've got my bike, but thanks!" I smile and wave.

Corndog nods slowly. He looks a bit sad. "Have a good night then!"

"Someone's got a crush on Parker," Brian says in a sing-song tone only I can hear.

"Shut up, you." I'm tempted to slap his arm playfully, but Laura and Allie are here and I'm sure they're looking this way. Do they suspect anything? Do they know I want Brian bad?

One thing's for sure: any problem can be solved with a big slobbery dog named Brandy.

• • •

The sun is low and the sky is a dark blue when I lock my bike, shove my hands in my jacket pockets, and skip toward the stream.

I stroll along the creek, admiring the tall green reeds sticking out of the water. Rocks and mud line the banks. I keep an eye out for frogs and turtles and lizards and snakes—I'd like to see them. I toss a few stones in the water.

A dog barks, and I lift my head to find Brian coming my way, being pulled by a big black lab. I glance around quickly to make sure we're alone, then rush toward them.

He's wearing flip flops, worn jeans, and a faded Titans sweatshirt. No cap—his black wavy hair hangs loose. I want to weave my fingers into it.

"Hey," I say to Brian. I get down on one knee, feeling mud soak through my jeans, and start scratching Brandy's ears and kissing her face. "You are gorgeous," I tell the dog. I hug her neck and pat her back and she barks and paws at me and wags her tail. "You are the sweetest."

"Thanks," Brian says, smiling down at me, the leash wrapped tightly around his fist.

"I was talking to Brandy. Duh."

Brian squats and rubs Brandy's neck while staring at my face. "This is much better than hanging out in a janitor's closet."

"I'm fine with hanging out wherever." I look in his eyes.

"Want to walk?"

"Sure," I say, bouncing to my feet. Brandy jumps, and her paws get muddy prints on my pink shirt.

"Brandy, behave, girl!" Brian exclaims, securing her leash. His eyes run over the dirt on my clothes. "Sorry…"

I wave a hand. "Can I hold her leash?" He hands it to me. Brandy jumps up again, to try to lick my face and I say, "Good dog."

"Someone's got a fan," Brian says.

Brandy hauls me down to the water and starts drinking. Then she hops in and splashes around the rocks. "Brandy, be careful! There are snakes in there."

Brian appears beside me and plays with my shirt sleeve. My heart beats like crazy. I have to control my breathing.

"You're hilarious, you know that?" he asks.

"I *am* Elaine."

He lifts his eyebrows, so I go on to tell him about how I play Elaine for Drew, Corndog, and Sam sometimes, and that makes Brian laugh so hard.

"So you go sit at Jiffy Burger and talk about nothing?" he asks, grinning like a madman.

"Don't make fun of me!"

"I'm not, it's funny. I totally would've done that in high school."

"When you weren't in detention or suspended, you mean."

"You got me."

We wander by the creek, and Brian picks up sticks and rocks to lob into the water. The air is perfect—cool, with a dash of spring. For a while we don't talk. We listen to the wind and Brandy's barking and slobbering. Soon we're under a bridge. The concrete supports are covered by colorful graffiti like "I'm an audio pirate!" and "Crips" and "AW + TG."

Brandy tugs on her leash, pulling me forward.

"I think that's enough, Brand," Brian says, taking her leash back. His fingers graze my skin before he squats down to whisper to his dog.

Aside from nudging me or playing with my shirt and other meek attempts at flirting, he hasn't made a move. Do I have to wear the pants? I peek down at his face—pensive, as he pets her black coat.

I thrust my hand toward him. He looks at it, then at my eyes before taking it and standing. I lace my fingers with his. The wind gently threads through his black hair.

"Parker…I don't want you to get the wrong idea—"

"What idea?"

He looks at our hands again, then strokes mine with a thumb. It feels so good I moan softly like I did that day in class. Only this time, I'm a hell of a lot more embarrassed.

"What idea?" I press.

"This." He holds up our entwined hands. "It's not a good idea."

He's right, it's wrong, and I should care, but I don't. And I tell him as much. His eyes grow wide. I keep moving closer to him, and he doesn't run or jump into the river or anything, so I squeeze his hand tighter. Brandy jerks her leash, trying to pull Brian away from me. His gaze never leaves mine as he says, "Brandy, come on, girl. Sit."

The dog collapses at his feet, and Brian secures the leash around his hand as I put my hands on his hips. He shudders. With his free hand, he touches my hair and laughs softly at my tangles. The thumping of my heart threatens to drown out Brandy's panting and the sound of water lapping over rocks.

I get up on tiptoes and stroke his stubble. I glance at his lips, then at his eyes. He's focusing on my mouth. He digs fingers into my hip. Now or never.

"Brian."

My mouth finds his, and I wrap my arms around his neck. He pulls back at first, gasping, his breath warm against my lips. He dives back in. His chapped lips feel rough against mine. He pushes me up against the concrete bridge support. The stone scrapes my lower back. I deepen the kiss. His tongue explores inside my mouth. My knees go wobbly. My breathing quickens, and I'm clutching his shoulders and holding on tight so I don't fall.

He yanks away from me.

"What's wrong?" I whisper, panting.

"Nothing, nothing." He touches his lips. "I had fun today. See you around?"

"You're leaving?" I blurt.

"I need to change the oil in Mom's car, and I have to pay some bills and work on some insurance paperwork."

He stopped kissing me so he can go work on insurance?!

Was I not a good enough kisser? Is he not interested in me? "Insurance? Really?"

His face is all red, and he clutches the back of his neck. "I need to go before I do something we'll regret."

"I won't regret anything!" I say, but he's already moving away quickly. He leads Brandy back to his truck, leaving me here with nothing but dark rushing water.

• • •

This makes two Saturday nights in a row I haven't gone out to find someone to kiss. I guess I really like Brian. I'm repainting my fingernails when I get a text from Corndog:

Look out ur window!

I peek outside and find him and Drew standing in the front yard, waving. I go let them inside, and Corndog says, "Let's go to Jiffy Burger. I need a Monster burger."

"You know, those things have, like, a thousand calories," I reply, blowing on my wet nails. My pinky is smudged already.

"A thousand calories? Really?" Corndog smiles. "I could eat two of those burgers and meet my caloric intake needs for the day."

"Exactly," Drew responds, bumping Corndog's fist.

"You in?" Corndog grins coyly at me.

"Okay," I reply. Anything to take my mind off Brian and his kisses. And his insurance paperwork, for crying out loud.

As we drive the streets of Franklin, I watch for Brian's truck. He's not at Freddie's Oyster Bar. He's not at the Barnes and Noble. He's not at the Porno Supermarket (thank the heavens!). He's nowhere. I check my phone to see if he texted—maybe I didn't hear the chime over Drew's rap music.

I'm such a psycho. He's twenty-three! We can't have anything. Why would he risk his reputation, risk everything, by dating a student? Even if we wait until after I graduate, I'll still be six years younger and in a totally different universe of meal plans and being sexiled out of my dorm room and not worrying about insurance. I haven't even gone to college, and he's probably worried about buying matching furniture and starting a 401K. He's spending his Saturday night paying bills! Holy boring.

"Parker? Parker?" Corndog shakes my knee. I jerk my head. He's been trying to get my attention from the front seat apparently.

"Sorry, I was thinking."

"What about?" Corndog asks.

"What do you think about matching furniture?"

He grins. "It's supposed to match?"

"Doesn't your mom's furniture match?"

He shrugs, then thinks for a long moment, drumming his fingers on his thighs. "I was thinking about what toppings I should get on my Monster burger."

"Oh yeah?"

"Yeah. I'm not getting tomatoes this time. They make the bread soggy. But I love tomatoes, so maybe I'll ask them to put some on the side for me? And I like pickles, but I don't like them mixed with mustard, so I'll probably ask for those on the side too."

I tsk tsk. "Picky, picky."

"What are you getting on your Monster burger?"

"I can't eat that. It has tons of calories and carbs."

He flicks the back of my hand. "C'mon. You can afford to cut loose a little."

"If I was going to get toppings, I'd get mayo and lettuce. I agree with you about the tomatoes. I think they take away from the taste of the burger. I like dipping my fries in mayo."

"Me too!"

"Are y'all gonna ignore me the whole night?" Drew asks from behind the wheel.

"Uh, yeaaaah," I reply. "Besides, you're obviously all dressed to

125

impress somebody." I point at his skinny jeans. He's been wearing them a lot lately.

"Hear, hear," Corndog mutters.

"Shut up, man," Drew replies. He fixes his hair with one hand.

At Jiffy Burger, aka Monk's (per Corndog's instructions, when we are inside JB we have to call it Monk's like on *Seinfeld*. Boys are ridiculous.), the guys get in line while I stake out our usual booth by the fingerprint-covered window.

"What do you want to eat, Parker?" Corndog calls out.

"Nothing," I reply, and he gives me a look. "Fine, I'll take a Diet Coke." He grins and holds my gaze for a few seconds. Then my phone buzzes.

Brian's text reads: What are u doing?

Out at JB w/ guys.

Corndog?

Yeah, he's here

….

Jealous?

….

He's a friend

Good to know

Don't go all stalker on me LOL :)

:) Can we talk?

Later—I'm out w/ friends

I slide my phone shut and put the ringer on silent. I'm still processing what happened this afternoon. I made out with a twenty-three-year-old guy! He kissed me and ran! He's acting all jealous. All in one day! Normally, I'd just say to heck with him, but boy can he kiss. He makes my body crackle like a firework. We connect. And I like him. I really like him. My heart surges and I grin.

"What are you smiling at?"

I look up to find Tate standing there…with Aaron and Laura, fused at the hip. It's not like I was into Aaron, but I hate that Laura's here flaunting that she could get what I once had.

Seeing them together and being here with Corndog reminds me of the eighth grade homecoming dance. Laura and I went together. Corndog was pretty dorky back then—always pushing his glasses up on his nose, always hiking his jeans up because he was skinny. But I was a nice Christian girl, and when he asked me to be biology partners, I said okay. *We'll make a good grade together*, I thought. At the dance, he was there hanging out with Drew, but Drew had plenty of girls to dance with, while Corndog stuck to sitting on a radiator on the side of the cafeteria. When Laura went to the bathroom, I leaned against the radiator and talked to Corndog about our science fair project. We wanted to know if different kinds of water affect the growth of plants, and so far my rainwater was making our dandelions grow faster than his Little Duck River water. We laughed about that, and he looked me in the eyes and asked me to dance.

"Sure," I replied, and in the middle of the cafeteria, under dimmed lights, he set his trembling hands on my waist and I smiled up at him.

I remember JJ walking by, smacking his butt, and saying, "Corndog, you dog, you. Good for you, man."

Corndog blushed, and smiled, and said to me, "Sorry about that."

"No biggie."

His hands kept shaking. "JJ said that 'cause you look really pretty tonight."

"Thanks," I said, grinning. The song ended, and Corndog wiped his palms on his jeans and rocked from foot to foot, and that's when Laura stormed up and asked him to dance. He glanced at me, but said yes to her, and by the end of the dance, Laura had a major crush on Corndog. But he didn't want to date her. Frankly, he seemed scared, shuffling away any time she came near.

Laura said it was my fault he didn't like her, and that if I was a good friend, I'd hate him along with her. After that, I kept away from him, for Laura's sake. I could never hate somebody, but we never partnered on projects again. We battled it out over grades. And now here we are tonight, together at Jiffy Burger.

"What are you guys doing here?" I ask, fidgeting in my seat.

"Eating Monster burgers, obviously," Tate says with a grin. He holds up a brown sack.

"I don't know who your friend is," Drew says, sliding past Tate into the seat across from me. He pops a fry in his mouth and speaks as he chews. "But I like him. Any friend of the Monster burger is a friend of mine."

Tate raises his eyebrows at Drew and smiles.

Corndog slips into the booth next to me and starts pulling burgers and cartons of fries out of the greasy paper sack. Holy calories. My stomach grumbles.

Aaron throws Corndog the same look Brother John wears anytime someone mentions Satan. "Is this guy why you never answered my calls?" Aaron turns his glare to me.

Laura grasps his elbow, looking horrified. Her eyes dart back and forth between Aaron and Corndog.

"This is my friend, Corndog," I say to Aaron and Tate. I introduce everyone, and Corndog shifts in the seat next to mine, glancing from me to Aaron.

Drew asks, "Do y'all want to join us?"

Tate replies, "I'd love to, but we already bought tickets to see *Fat Momma's House 6*...See you at church tomorrow?" He's speaking to me, but his eyes shift back to Drew.

"See ya then," I say with a wave, and they head for the exit. Laura slips an arm around Aaron's waist, but he edges away. Tate points at them and then looks back at me and laughs, rolling his eyes. She's never been very nice to Tate either. One time he attached a peace sign charm to his shoelace, and she went on and on about how the peace sign is a common devil worshipping sign. Hell, I bet the JB emblem is a devil worshipping sign. Thou shalt not eat Monster burgers!

I clear my throat. "I know those guys from church."

After a long silence, Corndog unwraps a burger, then slides it in front of me. I stare down at the burger. Lift the bun. It has mayo and lettuce only. Just how I would've asked for it. Then he gives me a carton of fries with a little cup of mayo for dipping.

"Eat up," he says.

"Thank you." I kind of want to cry.

He grins. "Sure thing."

I bite into my burger and wipe the juice from my lips. Chew. Right then, being here with these two guys, everything is perfect.

That's when Drew decides to tell the truth.

open
37 days until i turn 18

Drew finishes swallowing a fry, takes a deep breath, then looks up at me. "Is your friend Tate dating anybody?"

I suck air in. "I don't think so. He hasn't mentioned anyone."

"Why?" Corndog asks, crinkling his forehead.

Drew suddenly buries his eyes in the heels of his hands. I meet Corndog's face as recognition sets in for him. Corndog grabs my fingers under the table and squeezes hard.

What do I say?!

I don't want Drew to think I'm judging him. I don't know why, but I know how to play this.

"Wait a minute. Tate's gay?" I ask.

Drew pokes his face out from behind his hands. "I think."

"I had no idea." I eat a fry and talk as I chew. "How do you know?"

"I can just tell."

Corndog smoothes his hair and glances at me sideways. I let go of his fingers and reach across the table and take Drew's hand in mine, to show I love him. His eyes find mine, and I can tell he knows I knew.

"Why didn't you tell me?" Corndog asks.

"I just did." With his free hand he stuffs fries in his mouth. That's when Corndog reaches across the table and puts his hand on top of ours.

"I'm glad you said something," I reply.

"Is this staying a secret?" Corndog asks. "Or are you going to tell other people?"

"I don't know yet," he croaks. His breathing quickens. "I'm not even sure...I mean, I like girls too. Sometimes, I mean. I—"

"It's okay," Corndog says. "Let us know if we can do anything."

"Why are you guys huddling in Jiffy Burger?" Sam calls out, striding up to our table.

Drew quickly wiggles his hand out from under ours and takes a big bite of his burger, getting ketchup and mustard on his chin. He wipes his mouth with the back of his hand and burps. Nice front. I guess this is staying a secret for now. What a relief.

"You pig," I say. "Don't choke on your Monster burger."

"Did someone say Monster burger?" JJ says from behind Sam.

"Nasty," Joe Carter says.

"Where's Jordan tonight?" I ask Sam.

"She kicked me out," he says with a laugh. "She's with Carrie and Marie at some party. We're going to crash it in a few. Y'all want to come?"

"I'm in," Drew says, dusting salt off his hands.

After I watch the guys eat, like fifty thousand Monster burgers, we drive to Kristen Markum's house, where lots of people are crowded in the dark living room, dancing to rap music and sipping beer. She's a nasty piece of work and lots of people dislike her, but hey, a party's a party, I guess.

"I'm here!" Sam yells and hurtles himself into the mix.

"Woo!" Drew hollers, following him into the throng of girls

huddled near a beer pong table. I watch as he takes a shot directly out of a Smirnoff bottle and wipes his mouth, then does another shot. He passes the bottle to Sam, who takes a swig.

JJ and Carter meet up with their girlfriends, leaving me alone with Corndog. He slips a hand onto my lower back.

"Want a drink?" he asks.

"I don't really drink."

"Me neither." He seems deep in thought and looks around the room. His hand doesn't leave my back. It makes me feel safe.

Laura doesn't come to parties—she's a Christian, after all—so it doesn't surprise me that she's not here with Aaron and Tate, but Allie is here, checking me out. Hypocrite. Some guy has his arms around her and she's grinding her butt against him.

"Don't you know who I am?" I hear Drew yell. Some laughing sophomores—very popular sophomores—are backing him into a corner. One girl whips out a roll of duct tape. Another shoves him against the wall and French kisses him. "I'm the star of the football and baseball teams—you can't do this to me!"

"This oughta be good," Corndog says, crossing his arms and smiling. The warm spot on my back where his hand had been goes cool.

A minute later, the girls have gotten JJ to lift Drew off the ground, and they duct tape his wrists and ankles to the wall. He's hanging there like a fly stuck in honey.

"Didn't know that was possible," I say, wide-eyed.

"Do you want to find someplace quiet?" Corndog asks over the music. "To talk?"

I've never felt comfortable at parties. "Can we leave?"

He grins, and we go tell Drew we're taking off. He's still hanging on the wall.

"I think I'll head home," I say, faking a yawn.

"Me too," Corndog says, touching my back again. "I'll make sure she gets home, okay?" he says to Drew, who looks from me to Corndog. Sadness washes over his face.

I get up on tiptoes and give Drew a hug—well, the best hug I can considering he's totally spread eagle.

"Take care of him," I tell Sam, who's standing nearby with Jordan, nuzzling her neck. She's smiling at Sam sideways.

"You got it," he replies. I can trust him to peel Drew off the wall and get him home safely.

Then Corndog and I take off walking down the highway, passing the Franklin Public Library and Rose Jewelers.

"Well this was a stupid idea," I say, once I realize it's freezing outside. Must be in the fifties.

"I'd offer you my coat, but I don't have one."

"You could offer me your shirt." I laugh, pointing at his long-sleeved tee.

"But then we'd look like total white trash. Me walking down the street all bare-chested."

"I'll still be your friend, even if you look like white trash."

He laughs and stuffs his hands in his pockets. "Thanks, that means a lot. I think." He pauses as a semi races past us, kicking up dust and gravel. He shields me from most of the debris. The dust makes me cough, and he pats my back. We continue on down the highway, and every time a car gets near us, I yell, "Ahhh, Corndog, save me!" and bury my face in his shoulder so I don't get a mouthful of rocks.

"Why won't you call me Will?" he asks.

"I dunno. You've always been Corndog. My archrival."

He focuses on the pavement. "Not anymore. You won valedictorian."

"I did."

"But you're still thinking of me as your archrival."

"I'm Princess Peach, and you're Bowser," I say with a laugh.

"You think I'm an ugly dinosaur-dragon dude who kidnaps women for fun?"

"It's better than being a plumber like Mario. At least Bowser has all those castles. He's rich!"

"So it's all about money for you?"

Right there on the side of the road, I do a little line dance. "Any man of mine's gotta give me lots of presents."

He pulls me into a waltz. "Oh yeah? Like what?"

"Nail polish? iTunes gift certificates?"

"A guy doesn't have to be rich to manage that. I can definitely afford to buy nail polish." Will twirls me.

"I can't wait to tell all the guys you're gonna buy me nail polish."

"Don't!" he blurts. We laugh so hard, dancing stupidly in a circle.

We mosey past Advanced Auto Parts. Will says, "Crazy what happened with Drew. I didn't know."

"I had a feeling. I'm surprised he finally told me."

"Why?"

Will supported Drew tonight when he told us his secret, so I decide to tell the truth, even though it makes me feel a bit like I'm standing on a cliff with a strong wind at my back. "Because of everything with my mom."

"What about your mom?"

I pause. "You don't know about my mom?"

His face is blank. "Nope. Your parents are divorced, right?"

"You don't remember what happened last year? You don't remember all those rumors that Laura spread around?"

He musses his hair, looking confused. "Nope."

He never knew about my mom? He and Drew never discussed it? If he doesn't know, who else doesn't know? That means Will doesn't understand why I fool around with so many guys, that I want to show people I'm not like my mother. He probably thinks I'm just a slut. That day at baseball practice, he told me that I keep screwing with his friends. My reputation must be complete shit. And all for nothing.

This isn't what I want for myself. I want a normal life, a life where I won't be afraid of people letting me down. I squat by the side of the road and cover my face, letting a few tears trickle out. Will kneels next to me and rests his hands on my knees.

"What's up, Parker?"

The story tumbles out. What happened with Mom and Dad. What happened with Laura. Why I quit softball. I squeeze Corndog's hand, wanting him to pull me out of the wind.

"That sucks…Listen, I'm so sorry about what happened with Laura and softball and school, but your parents still love you, right?"

I wipe my nose with the heel of my hand and sniffle. "Um, I hardly ever talk to Mom. And Dad is like a zombie who thinks prayer solves everything. And my brother is all messed up on drugs."

"Why don't you talk to your mom?"

"Because she messed everything up," I whisper. "She caused my church to turn on me." I give him a rundown of what happened.

"Your church turning on you doesn't sound very Christian-like to me," he says, rubbing the side of his neck.

"I know…Church used to be so important to me…and after that, I didn't know who I was anymore."

A semi roars by, so I shut my eyes to shield them from dust. Will runs a hand over my head and then lifts my chin. "You're a great girl." He pulls me to my feet. "I'm sure your mom feels terrible about what happened. Is she okay?"

I pause, listening to the sound of cars rushing by. I don't know if she's okay. I've been so worried about myself and Dad and Drew and Ryan that I haven't even considered Mom's feelings. I'm a hypocrite. I worried about how Drew would feel, if he came out, but never thought about how it affected Mom. Does she feel bad for leaving Dad? Does she feel guilty?

Does she feel alone?

Does she hurt because she lost her family too? Because we left her like she left us? I was ready and willing to support Drew, but not my own mother. The memory of the day I found her cooking a roast while crying screams in my mind.

Tears trickle down my face, and Will wipes them away with his shirt sleeve. "I'm so mad at God. For doing this to my family."

"It's like you said," Will whispers. "Shitty stuff happens sometimes. I'm angry at God right now too, because of Bo."

We start trudging down the highway again, soon turning onto my street behind the KFC.

"Maybe you should come to my church sometime," he says.

"Where do you go?"

"Westwood."

"I'd be up for that." I'm enjoying walking with him. Going slowly gives me time to think.

"Maybe tomorrow?" he asks softly, as we approach my house. The porch light splashes onto the grass and sidewalk.

"I'd like that."

"What are you gonna do about your mom?"

I shake my head and yawn. "I can't think anymore tonight." I don't even know what I'd say if I were to call Mom. I'm too embarrassed. Too ashamed. Too hurt. I can't sort it out in my mind.

He drags a hand through his hair and studies my face. "Thanks for telling me that stuff."

"You can pour your heart out to me next time," I joke.

"Maybe I will tomorrow after church." He laughs. "We can watch another chick flick."

Part of me wonders if Brian will want to hang out tomorrow, while another part of me wants to spend time with Will.

"Sounds good."

He squeezes my hand before hopping off the porch. "I'm picking the movie this time, though."

• • •

Before doing anything, I send Drew a text: Are you off the wall?

Barely.

Drunk?

I drank sooo much. Will be sick for days. :(

:(Thx for telling me about u. Love u.

Love u too. Nice time w/Corndog?

Very nice. Good friend.

Only a friend?

Yeah…

I like him

Oh no, I think. Drew must be way drunk. I text back: You *like* like Corndog?

For a long time. Pls don't tell him! I just wanted to tell somebody!

I won't tell. No worries.

Thx. Love u.

I slide my phone shut. Stare at it. Drew likes Will. After Drew broke up with Amy, he told Will he was interested in someone else. Shit.

I wash and moisturize my face and brush my teeth. All the while thinking of Will and how fun tonight was, and how now that I know how Drew feels, I'm like a balloon that's been popped and the air is rushing out, leaving nothing but confusion.

Once I'm in bed, I think of Brian. He said he wanted to talk, so I take a deep breath and call him. He picks up on the first ring. "Hey." He sounds tired and relieved. "I was worried about you."

"I'm fine...so this afternoon..." I curl up under my covers while waiting for his response.

"It was...nice."

"I thought so too—"

"It can't happen again."

"I don't get that. We'll keep it a secret."

"You're so young..." He pauses for a long moment. "It's hard to keep away from you. My job's on the line. My future. I could get in a hell of a lot of trouble for what happened today, Parker. Have you thought of that?"

"Sorta..."

"Just sorta? You have to take responsibility for stuff as an adult."

"I thought you were living for today or whatever."

"I'm trying. But I'd rather live for today and not lose my job for kissing a student."

"I'm only going to be a student for another couple of months, you know."

"I know, I know." He takes a deep breath. "This is hard for me right now, okay? My mind's messed up."

"'Cause of baseball?"

"Yeah. I thought I'd make it to the big leagues and now I'm stuck—" He stops.

"You can talk to me."

"I want to, but I need time to figure this out."

"What's there to figure out?"

"I like you, okay? I like you. But I don't know how to deal. I don't really want to sneak around. I'm not like that."

"Who says we have to sneak around? Give it a month and it'll be legal. I'll be eighteen."

"That doesn't make it right."

Today's kisses seemed right to me.

"I want to see you," I tell him.

He exhales deeply. Hesitates. "Now?"

I glance at my watch. 11:30 p.m. Dad is definitely asleep. Ryan probably passed out listening to his strange trance music.

"Now," I say.

He says he'll meet me at the laundromat across the road in twenty minutes. Perfect! Gives me time to take a quick shower. After doing my powder and lip gloss, I slip on black underwear, velvet sweatpants, and a matching hoodie. Then I click the front door shut and dart across the street, shivering under the streetlights. I'm glad Ryan's window faces the backyard.

The laundromat is closed, so Brian's truck is the only vehicle in sight, tucked behind the Dumpsters. Away from the streetlights. He smiles through the window and waves, his eyes darting around. I open the door to his truck, slide across the bench and kiss him before he can stop me. He tastes like mint toothpaste. My hands are on his neck and his are in my hair, and I can tell he's experienced. He's probably had sex.

He pushes me backward and climbs on top, his weight heavy, yet comforting.

This is way different than with other guys.

• • •

Every Halloween, my church puts on a morality play, usually where the teenage characters get sloppily drunk and don't treat their bodies like temples, or have sex before marriage, and end up going to Hell. People who come to watch the play walk through a room made to look and feel like Hell. A Judgment House. We crank up the heat to 100 degrees. Red Christmas lights act as burning embers in the bowels of Hell. A soundtrack featuring a weird demon-devil creature cackling plays in the darkness. Sure, people made fun of the depiction of Hell, but it always scares me because I know the real Hell must be a million times worse.

God, is my family going to end up there? Because we're sinners?

Written before church on February 28. Burned, using a match.

• • •

I whip open the front door to find Will, here to collect me for church.

"Hey, come on in," I say, grinning.

"Thanks." He's wearing khakis, a blue shirt and tie, and loafers. He rubs his palms together.

"Let me just get my bag." I skip to the bathroom and check my lip gloss and powder one more time before grabbing my purse from my bed. Instead of leather boots, I slip my feet into heels. When I go back to the foyer, Dad's standing there pinching his bottom lip. I picked up that habit from him.

"You're going to another church?" Dad asks, furrowing his brow.

"Yeah. Is that okay?" I ask, pulling a jacket on over my simple pink dress.

Dad sets a hand on Will's shoulder and studies his face. "What church do you go to, Corn Fritter?"

I crack up. "It's Corndog!"

Will covers a laugh with his fist. "I go to Westwood, sir."

Dad turns his attention back to me. "I, uh, is there something wrong with our church?"

"Just wanted to spend time with my friend."

Will beams at that, but I shrug, acting like going to another church is no big deal, even though it kinda is. I've never been anywhere but Forrest Sanctuary.

Dad takes longer than an inning to come up with a response. "This is a one-time thing, right? You'll be back at our church for WNYG and services next Sunday?"

"Definitely," I say, then I'm pulling Will out the front door by his wrist. We climb into his truck, and he whistles.

"You sure got a strong grip." He rubs his wrist, chuckling. "I'm glad I'm not a ball bat."

I laugh softly. "And I'm out of shape."

Will inserts his key into the ignition and turns it; the diesel engine rumbles to a start. "I'd be happy to bat or throw a ball around with you anytime," he says, pulling onto the highway. A milk truck passes us.

We ride to Westwood in a comfortable silence filled only by the soft crooning of Rascal Flatts. He has a picture of Bo and two other boys tucked against the glass above his odometer. Must be his brothers. We grin at each other.

"I wish we hadn't competed all through school," I say. "I wish we had been friends before now."

"Yeah." He focuses on the road.

We pull into the church parking lot, and even though it's February and freezing, people our age are either playing a game of pick-up basketball or cheering the players on. Will is out of the car and jogging toward the guys before my seatbelt is unbuckled.

He jets to center court, steals the ball from some guy, and shoots, nailing two points. It makes me smile, but I'm also kinda pissed he abandoned me in the car. But before I flip out, he's jogging back over, his brown hair flopping across his forehead. He whips open my door and helps me step out, then leads me over to the courts. Only about twelve kids are here—a lot fewer than at Forrest Sanctuary. I recognize two people: Asshole Paul Briggs the catcher, and Jenna—a sophomore who plays center field for the softball team. She's killer at bat. She gives me a little wave.

"Go say hi," Will tells me. "I'll introduce you around after I play some ball." He runs off to steal the basketball again.

I take a deep breath and go see Jenna.

"Love your dress," she says, scanning me.

"You too," I reply. She's wearing a cute gray dress. It looks vintage.

"You're here with Will?" she asks, bouncing a little.

"Yep."

"He's never brought a girl to church before."

"Yeah?"

Jenna nods, and proceeds to talk my ear off about softball and her crush on some sophomore named Tim Keller who I've never heard of, and she starts quizzing me about Will and who he's dating. I shrug and watch as Will dodges Paul to bank a layup off the back-board. The ball swooshes through the net.

I clap and go, "Wooo!"

Will tosses the ball to some guy and heads toward me with a blazing smile on his face. "Sorry. Couldn't help but show off a bit. Want to come inside and meet my mother?"

"Um, sure." I tell Jenna it was nice talking to her, then follow Will inside what must be their Fellowship Hall. Will holds my elbow as we stride up to a beautiful woman drinking coffee while playing with her necklace, a chain holding a single pearl. She's in her forties and has very structured brown hair, like she's in a Lands' End catalog or something. When he touches her shoulder, the woman stops talking and turns.

"You must be Parker," she says, sticking out a manicured hand. Her nails are a deep maroon.

"Yes, ma'am," I reply. She checks out my nails too. Today I wore Blushingham Palace, a soft pink to match my dress. She releases my hand, then looks back up.

"I'm Mrs. Whitfield." Ah. A true Southern belle. Those kind of women at my church give me total stink eye.

"Nice to meet you, ma'am," I say, giving her a nervous smile.

"You too, dear." She sips her coffee. "I've been wanting to meet the girl who's smarter than my Wills."

"Mom," Will whines. "Would you stop calling me Wills? It makes me sound like I'm royalty or something."

She sticks out her pinky finger and waves her Styrofoam cup in an aristocratic manner. "Well you are my little prince."

His eyes bulge and his mouth falls open. "Mom. Stop."

She smiles and wraps an arm around his waist. "Hush. You know I've been wanting you to bring around a respectable girl."

My face heats up, and I can't help but grin. Respectable. This is new and different. If the women at my church could keep their sons on a different continent than me, they would.

Will goes to get me some water and leaves me to chat with his mother, who's thrilled to hear I'm planning on going to Vanderbilt. He comes back carrying bottled water for me in one hand and Bo in the other arm.

"You remember my brother, Bo," Will says, looking at him proudly. Will squeezes Bo's knee, and I'm overcome by how jealous I am of that love. "Can you say hi to Parker?"

Bo buries his face in Will's shoulder.

"Hey, Bo," I say. "You love baseball, right?"

He peeks up and nods, and Mrs. Whitfield raises her eyebrows at Will.

Later, Will introduces me around. I say hi to Marie Baird from school, and she says she's glad I came to church today. And then Will's youth pastor, this huge guy named Lance, shakes my hand like a rattle.

"Welcome to Westwood," he says. "It's Game Sunday."

"Game Sunday?" I ask.

"We clear the tables out of this room and the youth play games. Today we're gonna play Freeze Tag and Red Rover for sure." Lance shuffles off.

"Freeze Tag is a terrible idea," Will murmurs to me.

"Does he not notice that y'all aren't five anymore?" I whisper.

"Lance is the king of terrible ideas."

Lance begins moving furniture as the adults and younger children clear out of the room. Soon it's only people our age. Jenna is flirting with some boy while Paul keeps touching Marie and she keeps batting him away.

Loud Christian rock music tumbles out of the speakers. The drums make the windows vibrate. Funny. Brother John once told us that "heavy drum music makes teenagers act in sinful ways," so we shouldn't listen to it.

Will takes the water out of my hand and sets it on a window sill as Lance yells, "Tag, you're it!" and slaps a younger boy's arm. All the girls kick their heels off, so I do too. We start running, slipping on the linoleum floor, and I'm laughing like crazy. The boy tries to tag me, but I sidestep him and speed across the room.

"Nice," Will calls out to me.

The boy takes off after Jenna and tags her. To unfreeze her, Paul tries to crawl through her legs and she's hollering "Gross! Stop! Stop!" and batting him away.

"Paul! You're three times her size!" Lance calls out. He's trudging around the room at a turtle's pace.

"So?" Paul pauses right between her legs, and it's such a sight I stop running and I'm dying of laughter. Will is too.

"You think you can unfreeze her? You're like ten times the size of me," Paul says to Lance, who laughs.

The boy tags me, so I freeze. "Will! Come unfreeze me!"

He stops, finding my eyes. "Marie, help Parker!"

Marie comes and crawls through my legs, and I can't stop laughing. After my third game of Red Rover, I take a breather. Will joins me in sitting on the window sill; our feet bang against the wall.

"Why wouldn't you unfreeze me?" I ask, giggling.

He clears his throat. "I'm a lot bigger than you," he says, gesturing at his body. "Besides, it's not a very gentlemanly thing to do. I don't want to be like Pervy Paul over there."

"You're all right, Will Whitfield." I smile at him sideways.

He blushes, and gestures at his Fellowship Hall. "What do you think so far?"

"It's fun. But don't you have Bible Study? Or talk about good Christian behavior and whatnot?"

"Sure, sometimes," he replies, lifting a shoulder.

"You don't play games every week?"

He chuckles. "You're lucky you didn't visit on Don't Make Bad Life Choices Sunday."

"Don't Make Bad Life Choices Sunday?" I laugh.

"Yeah, Lance had a doctor come in and show us pictures of what lung cancer and STDs look like under a microscope."

My mouth drops open. "Sounds more effective than telling us we'll go to Hell if we get trashed or have sex before marriage."

Will's face wears a look of horror. "It was very effective. And then the doctor told us about the tests they run to find out if you have an STD." He swallows.

"I don't want to know."

"You definitely do not want to know." He glances at me, and his face goes even redder. But then he laughs. "Paul was freaking out."

"Waaaaay too much info, Will."

"Hey, if I had to suffer through it, so do you."

"You're evil."

"So do you want to watch *The Notebook* this afternoon?"

• • •

His mom invites me back to his house for Sunday lunch. She made baked chicken with lemon, corn on the cob, and cornbread. We hold hands while Mr. Whitfield says the Lord's Prayer. Will has two other brothers—Trey is nine and Rory is fourteen. Will and I open our eyes during the prayer, sneaking a quick smile at each other.

I love eating a home-cooked meal that I didn't have to make. And after that, Will and I collapse onto a couch in his basement and promptly fall asleep, like last Sunday. Only this time when I wake up, Will's head is resting on my shoulder and his hand is draped across my thigh.

A warm breeze rushes through my body, and I feel safe. Safe with him. His hand is on my leg and I find I like it being there.

What if Drew finds out? What if Brian finds out? How could I hurt Drew like that? How could I hurt Brian, who's risking everything for me?

Just goes to show that a trip to a new church won't automatically make me a good person. I don't deserve any of this.

Even if I like Will, and if by some miracle he wants me—which is kinda doubtful, considering how pissed he got that I was fooling around with his friends—I can't do this to Drew.

getting serious
36 days until i turn 18

No one except Tate calls to find out why I wasn't at church. Not Aaron, not Brother John, not Laura, not Allie. Will's right. They aren't very Christian. Only Tate called—not my cell, but my landline.

"I found your number in the church directory," Tate says.

"Hi, Parker!" I hear Rachel yell in the background.

He says, "I missed you today."

"I went to church with Will. You know, Corndog? From JB last night?"

"He seemed nice."

"He is. We just recently started hanging out." I tell Tate about how Will and I have been jostling for valedictorian for eons.

Tate asks, "Are you, um, interested in him?"

"My friend likes him," I say, sinking my head into a pillow. If Drew wasn't interested in him, and I wasn't messing around with Brian, and if Will and I hadn't been rivals all through school, would I be thinking way different thoughts about him? Yeah. But some hands don't always result in a full house. Sometimes you get two of a kind or an ace high. You don't get a royal straight flush including two happily married parents, a non-drug-using brother, and a big, slobbering dog, with none of your family members being deathly allergic to said dog.

"So Aaron's really with Laura?" I ask. I feel bad for hurting him, but I'm ashamed I kissed a guy who was so willing to try to make me jealous.

"For now. He doesn't like her like he likes you, though."

"I don't even get why he likes me." Why anybody likes me.

He clucks his tongue. "You're your own person. You wear what you want and don't bother with people who annoy you. Everyone wants to be like that."

What? Really? They think I don't bother with people who annoy me? It was Laura who started those rumors. It was the church ladies who started telling their children to keep away from me, for fear I'd turn out like Mom. Ladies who had once been Mom's friends.

But even if they did want to talk to me, would I want to talk to them? It's best to keep people away. Then I remember how I told Will everything last night. Everything. And he still took me to his church. He introduced me to his family.

"Parker? You there?" Tate says over the phone.

"Sorry, I was thinking."

"About?"

I pick at a loose thread dangling from my duvet. "Do you like our church?"

He chuckles. "Not much. The people are worse than Phillies fans."

"Harsh. You like baseball? I didn't know that."

"It's hard to talk about anything when we're always trying to stop Laura from convincing us to burn our iPods because we listen to Coldplay."

I pause. "Drew plays baseball for Hundred Oaks. Second base."

Tate exhales. The phone line crackles, as if he's breathing heavily. "Why've you never mentioned him before? Why'd you never bring him to church?"

"Why would I subject anyone to our church?" I say with a laugh. "And like you said, I was too busy trying to stop Laura from burning my iPod to mention friends from school."

"Ah."

Tate and I never really talked much before Mom left. Was he lonely? Has our church always made him feel uncomfortable with who he is? Is that why he started hanging out with me? Did he think I'd understand? I flip on my TV and start flicking through the channels, waiting for Tate to add something, but he doesn't.

I decide to tell a little lie, to get the conversation going again. "Drew said he thought you looked familiar."

"Really?"

"Yeah. Maybe you could look him up on Facebook?"

I hear crackling again. "I'll do that."

"His last name's Bates. Drew Bates."

"Cool. Thanks."

I'm grinning as we hang up. I lie back on my bed and decide not to repaint my nails.

• • •

Sunday night is *Veena Comes Over for Dinner*, take two. Dad gave me a warning this time so I can cook something good!

I'm using Gramma's hashbrown chicken casserole recipe, but I make it my own by switching out the Corn Flakes for Frosted Flakes. The sugar gives it a kick. I'm making a salad to go with it, so I'll have something to eat after my small portion of casserole.

"Smells good," Ryan says, coming into the kitchen.

"Thanks."

He takes a glass from the cabinet and pours himself some water. "What's the occasion?"

I rarely make this casserole, because it takes like two hours to put it together. "Dad's friend Veena is coming over."

Ryan pauses before sipping.

"She was really nice at dinner last week," I tell him, slicing into a cucumber. "I bet you'll like her. She's a nurse over at Murfreesboro Regional."

My brother doesn't answer, but he sits down at the table while I work. It surprises me that he's willing to keep me company.

I prepare a plate of cheese and crackers, which I push in front of him, making him smile a little. "Be right back," he says, disappearing. When he comes back, he's changed out of a T-shirt and into a navy blue polo shirt. If he'd cut his shaggy hair already, he'd look exactly like he did in high school, when so many girls liked him because he was so cute. I bet if Macy saw him in a polo shirt, she'd probably recite some Nietzsche quote and go on about how third-world children sew them in sweatshops, and then say if Ryan wears one, he's the harbinger of the apocalypse.

Then the apocalypse truly happens: Ryan helps set the table.

When Veena shows up, Dad answers the door. I peek around the wall into the foyer, to see them laughing quietly and chatting as he takes her jacket. Dad leans down and gives her a peck on the lips, which makes me wonder what they did after we went to Crockett's Roadhouse last week.

I can't stop smiling as we sit down to eat. Dad leads us in the Lord's Prayer, then we put our napkins in our laps and dig in.

"This looks really yummy," Veena says, forking up some casserole.

"Thanks," I reply.

"I haven't had a home-cooked meal since I left New York."

"Is your family there?" Ryan asks, salting his casserole.

"My parents, my sister and her husband, and my grandmother. And two nieces."

"You're a nurse?" Ryan asks her.

"Yep," she says, chewing.

"Did you always know that's what you wanted to do?"

She smiles, thinking. "I wanted to be an astronaut more, but I stink at math."

"It's my worst subject too," Ryan replies. "But I still want to go to med school."

"What programs are you thinking about?"

"Vanderbilt is one of the best, but I'm not enjoying my undergrad classes there."

She nurses her iced tea. "I didn't like mine either. I hated taking all those politics and English courses. And don't even get me started on art. But it's all a means to an end."

"Yeah, I get that," Ryan says. This is the most I've heard my brother speak in forever.

"If you want, we can get together for coffee this week sometime and talk more. Or you can come by the hospital and talk to some of the other doctors about what their undergrad experiences were like."

"That sounds good," Ryan replies, tapping his fork on his placemat.

Dad beams so hard he seems ten years younger.

It almost feels like a family, but I still wish Mom were here.

• • •

It's getting serious, yet it's staying the same. Every night this week I've made out with Brian. Ryan and Dad notice nothing, obviously, so it's no problem for me to sneak out of my room and dart across the street to Brian's parked truck tucked behind the Dumpsters after eleven.

On Monday night, we just kissed.

On Tuesday night, he went up my shirt.

On Wednesday at school, I stopped by Coach Lynn's office during study hall. Brian's squatting there until he gets his own office next year.

"What are you doing here?" Brian asked, slipping a pen behind his ear. He leaned back in his seat and wrapped his hands behind his head, smirking at me.

I waved a hall pass. "I nicked this from Mrs. Perkins. I wanted to see what you're up to."

He jumped to his feet, closed the door behind me, and locked it. I walked around the office, looking at Coach Lynn's things: silk roses in a vase, pictures of her family, the cat calendar on the wall.

"Love what you've done with the place."

"Smart ass," he replied, following me as I weaved around the desk and chairs. I wiped a finger across the desk, pretending to check for dust.

I knew it was wrong. All of it. Kissing him, and wanting to kiss him again. But when his arms are around me, everything feels good. I feel safe and cared for. And the kissing is very, very okay.

"So why did you stop by again?" He scratched the back of his neck and squinted.

I smiled mischievously. "I was in study hall and couldn't stop thinking about last night."

He closed the blinds. He breathed heavily. He ran a hand through his hair. He loosened his Best Buy Geek Squad tie. Then his lips were on mine and he lifted me onto the desk. He pulled my hips to his and kissed me until I was so dizzy I could barely breathe. Brian began to grind against me and I was so drunk on him, I couldn't think at all.

Then someone knocked on the door and Brian rushed to answer it, but stopped for a second to control his breathing. He motioned at me to fix my shirt. I leaped into the chair across from his desk. He opened the door to find Sam, who had dropped by to say he wouldn't be at practice that day because his mom was sick and his dad was out of town.

As soon as Sam left, Brian exhaled, mussed his black hair, and grinned. He moved toward me. I was shaking like crazy. He swept me up in his arms and gave me a quick kiss.

"That was insanely hot," he said.

"Yeah," I said with a tiny voice, trembling. Honestly? It was fun, but it filled me with shame. I hope God was looking the other way.

He went on, "But it can't happen again at school."

"I agree." Goose bumps popped up on my arms. I shuddered.

"We're okay." He pressed his forehead to mine and squeezed my hips. "You'd better get back to study hall before I give you detention."

Brian tried to joke it off, but I had seen the change on his face. What happened freaked him out too.

My face must've been blazing red, but Sam didn't say anything when I saw him later in chemistry.

On Wednesday night, Brian went up my shirt again and unsnapped my bra, and ran his hands over my bare breasts. Him running his calloused fingers over my skin took some getting used to because I couldn't stop trembling. But when I calmed down, we fell into a rhythm. A rhythm that kept getting faster and faster until our shirts and my bra ended up on the floorboard of the truck. I touched his abs, which I'm fairly certain are made of marble. His teeth sank into my shoulder, making me gasp. I discovered he has a tattoo on his shoulder blade. A symbol, but when I asked what it meant, he refused to tell me, saying it's private.

"Where's your tattoo?" he teased, trying to peek under my waistband. I smacked his chest and we laughed. But I couldn't stop thinking about that tattoo and what it means and why he couldn't share with me.

On Thursday night, he kissed my breasts and felt me through my jeans. I wasn't comfortable enough to touch him yet. But he took my fingers and put my hand there anyway.

A cold sweat tore over my body.

Then a cop knocked on the truck window and told us to move it along. I jumped out. Dashed into my house, to my room, panting and freaking out. My bra hung loose around my shoulders, and the top button of my jeans was undone. Brian called me when he got home. The whole thing upset him too.

But when I asked, "Can we go to your place instead of parking? I don't want to risk getting caught again," he replied, "We'll find another place to park."

"Why can't we go to your house?"

"Because I live above my parents' garage. What if they see you?"

"They don't have to know I'm seventeen. Just tell them I'm older."

"They might know you from church. I would be embarrassed if they found out about this."

"You're embarrassed by me?" I whispered.

"No, no. Just the situation would embarrass me. You're a student."

Even with my reputation, Will seemed proud of me at his church last Sunday. When he's lying on top of me, Brian seems pretty damned pleased with me.

"Sounds like you're embarrassed by me."

He sighed exaggeratedly. "Whatever."

"Could we go someplace else tomorrow night? Like dinner in Nashville?"

"That's not a good idea. We could get in a shitload of trouble. Who knows who might see us?"

"But making out in the parking lot across the street from my house is a good idea?" I really wanted to do something other than talk on the phone and make out in his truck. That used to be enough for me with other guys. But I'm starting to want the whole shebang, and the whole shebang should include going someplace…even Foothills Diner.

At the same time, my friendship with Will keeps getting better and better. Sometimes we walk together between classes, and two times this week he called me after practice.

Wednesday night, I lay on my bed, listening as he told me a story about how when he was three, he was so smart he figured out how to unlock the gate at his preschool's playground and he waddled down the street to McDonald's, where he walked in, clapped his hands and yelled, "Happy Meal!"

"Why don't you ever date?" I asked him quietly. Thinking of Drew, but also thinking of him. Him, and how my feelings for him were ballooning and floating off without my permission.

"Ehhhh," he said. "It's kinda silly, I guess. I never really felt like I knew who I was, and I was so into beating you at valedictorian, I didn't want that extra burden, especially considering my parents need help with Bo and the farm."

"I get that."

"I mean, I see the guys on the football and baseball teams who have girlfriends, and it's like…it's like it's their whole lives. I guess I want to have my own life first and then meet someone who can be a part of it…but not fill it…?"

"Huh," I replied, wiggling my toes at the ceiling. "Cool."

"What about you? Why don't you ever date?"

I'm sorta seeing your baseball coach…"Never wanted to get close to anyone. You know that."

"But you hook up."

"Yeah, but so do you," I replied, baiting him.

"Occasionally. But nothing serious."

"You mean…?" He hasn't done it yet?

"Yeah." He cleared his throat. "I'm not doing that until I'm in a real relationship."

"I'm a virgin too," I said quietly.

He paused for a long moment. "I didn't know that."

Then we went back to discussing the Prom Decisional. But it shocked me to know that Will, a hot eighteen-year-old baseball player and genius, was saving himself. It made me proud that I had saved myself too. Proud that I could tell him that.

During gym on Friday morning, Brian wouldn't even look my way as I ran around the track with Will. *Whatever*, I thought.

Brian blew his whistle. "I know you can go faster than that, Whitfield."

"What's up his ass today?" Will asked, not bothering to speed up.

"No idea," I replied, even though I knew. Brian doesn't like seeing me with Will.

"You talk to him a lot, right?"

I nearly stopped running, to freeze right there beside the goal post.

"Yeah, he's nice to me," I said, trying to sound nonchalant.

"He doesn't bother you, I hope."

I waved a hand. "No, no. We talk about stats and the Braves and stuff."

"Okay." Will stared over at Brian. Fear rushed through me. Had Sam mentioned finding us in Coach Lynn's office?

Back in the locker room, I overheard a couple girls saying that all I do in gym class is stare at Coach Hoffman, so I told myself not to look at him anymore.

But here I am on Friday night, making out with him in his truck. Dark and midnight. He touches me through my jeans and kisses me hard. The taste of bubble gum fills my mouth.

"You make me so hot," he says, pulling my leg to wrap around his waist.

It all feels so weird. I want it, yet I don't, but I'm not going to stop because it feels too good.

"I want to take this further," he says, gasping, pressing his hardness against my thigh. "But we need to wait until your birthday. Probably until after you graduate."

"Take this further how?" I reply, nibbling on his ear, making him groan and breathe faster.

His hand sneaks up my shirt. "You know, sleep together."

Okay, (1) We've only been making out for what, a week? (2) I'm a virgin. (3) That's pretty presumptuous, to think I'd automatically agree to sleep with him. Don't I get a say in any of this? We barely talk anymore. It's all kissing and disagreements, and while the kissing is yummy, my heart hurts.

"I'm not ready for that," I whisper, clutching his shirt.

He looks in my eyes before closing his. "Most people I know do it on the second or third date."

"Oh." I can't even imagine that. Some kids at school casually fool around, but I don't understand how they can get so intimate so quickly. To me, it seems like sex should happen naturally after a long period of dating and love. Not something that automatically happens because it's the third date. I guess this means Brian's had sex. Tons of it, probably, but I'm not gonna do the math.

"I'm not sure I want to." I avoid his eyes.

"It's fine," he mumbles before starting to kiss me again. His stubble scratches my chin. "Can we do something else, at least? For now?"

"What?"

"Will you…?" He unzips his jeans.

He wants me to put my mouth on it. "I can't," I gasp, ashamed at the thought.

"Can I touch you?" he whispers, unbuttoning my jeans. He slides them down my legs and stares at my lacy white underwear. I've never gone this far with a boy, and the look on his face is so sexy I tug on his jeans, revealing black boxer briefs. He pushes my panties aside, making me moan softly as he works a finger inside me.

Later I straddle him and he wraps his hands around my waist and we kiss and kiss, only thin cotton separating us. I get so caught up in wanting to know what this feels like with a man that I nearly forget he hasn't even taken me out on a real date yet.

"Next week, can we please do something outside of your truck?" I ask, delirious because of what he's doing to my neck.

"Really, it's not a good idea," he pants, slipping his hand back down my underwear.

I want to tell him he can't kiss away these issues, but somehow I doubt he'll hear me. I push his hand away and sit up, lifting my hips and pulling my jeans back on. The door handle wedges into my back. It's painful.

"I don't want to sleep with you in your truck," I say, licking my lips. They're chapped from kissing so much.

He weaves his fingers in my hair and presses his forehead to mine. "We wouldn't do it in my truck."

"But you won't let me go to your apartment now. Why will it be different in a month?"

"We can't go to my apartment. Ever."

"Fine." The windshield is fogged up.

He glances down at where my pants fasten, then leans back in. "We could go to a motel?"

"That's real classy."

"I don't mean to be a jerk…it's just I'm so scared about this." His breath feels hot against my face. His face wears a look of desperation. Like he wants me to follow his lead, no questions asked. "And sometimes I get so wrapped up in you and feeling like I'm young again, I forget about how much trouble we'll be in if anyone finds out."

I love that he's into me, but is he only into me so he'll "feel young again"? It's not like he's ancient. It's like the minute we started hooking up, he got scared, and the fear has changed him.

"I bet you'd take Coach Vixen back to your apartment," I say.

"You are Trouble, you know that?" he says with a laugh.

"It's not funny."

"I'm really into you, Park. I'm not interested in Jenna, I promise."

"I think I'm gonna go home." I start to open the door when Brian reaches out and pulls me into his arms.

"I'm sorry…We'll figure this out."

"You mean you'll figure this out. You won't listen to a single thing I say." I try to disentangle myself from his arms, but he holds me tighter.

"I'm trying." He leans his forehead against mine.

"I'm ready for bed." I'm so pissed, I don't bother with a good night kiss. "Bye."

"Good night." He sighs and drags a hand through his hair, and I climb out and trudge toward my house. Right as I step up to my porch, Drew emerges from the shadows. I gasp.

"Coach Hoffman? Really?" He looks freaked out. "You could get in so much trouble. What if your dad finds out? Or the school?" I hear Brian's truck squeal out of the laundromat parking lot.

"Oh my God. You can't tell!"

"I'd never do that. You know that."

"I know." I nod, closing my eyes. My body's shaking all over. Did Drew see us hooking up?

"But what about Corndog?"

"What about him?" I open my eyes to find Drew regarding me warily. Looking at me like he doesn't even know who I am.

"You know what I mean."

"Drew…" I clasp my hands. How do I tell him that even though Will's straight and will most likely never be interested in Drew back, I won't do that to him? I guess that's all I can say. "I'd never betray you. You're my best friend." I step closer to him and hug him around the waist, breathing in the comforting smell of lemons and cotton.

"Thanks," he chokes out. "But are you okay? I thought you just had a crush on him, but you're with him for real? Coach Hoffman? Really?"

"Would you stop saying 'Coach Hoffman? Really?'"

"How did this even happen?"

"It just did." My voice is tiny. "We probably won't last."

"Are you okay?"

I nod slowly.

"I won't deny that he's hot," Drew jokes. "But it's kinda pervy that he's into you."

I hug him tighter, but I'm wishing I was hugging Will. I feel like

I'm gonna barf. "Let's hang out tomorrow after the game, okay?" he says quietly.

"Okay." I release Drew and kiss his cheek. He heads toward his trailer down the street and I go to my room. I slide my cell open to find a slew of text messages from Brian and Will.

Brian's texts are: Does Bates know? Can he keep a secret?

Will's texts are: You busy tomorrow night? I have to babysit. Would love your company.

I change into pajamas and wash my face, daydreaming about Will coming through my window tonight, to hug me and make me feel safe and special.

Back in my room, I crawl under the covers and send Brian a text: All's okay. Good night.

I send Will a text: I'd like that.

A calm, cool response that doesn't betray Drew.

Even though it betrays my heart.

the mascot

Do I look different?

I'm staring at myself in the mirror.

I let Brian touch me, and I can't stop thinking about it. It's not like I lost my virginity or anything, but I feel like I gave away part of me. I turn sideways and examine my figure, arching my back, making sure I look slim in my jeans and navy blue cotton long-sleeved shirt. Cute for today's game. But I'm not sure who I'm trying to look cute for. I'm not sure it's Brian anymore, and I shouldn't want to look pretty for Will. Honestly, I doubt Will would care that my lip gloss is perfect and my nails aren't chipped.

I drag a hand through my hair, my fingers shaking. Drew saw me with Brian…and I'm not proud of it. I blow air out, trying to breathe evenly.

I'm not totally sure why, I guess I got caught up in it—in him, but last night after Brian touched me, I felt him too. He shut his eyes and leaned his head back against the seat while my fingers moved up and down. I could tell by the noises he made that he liked how I made him feel, but it was almost as if I could be anybody. It didn't matter who I was, it was only that somebody was giving him pleasure.

I don't want to be just anybody.

I want to matter, to be loved. I want the real.

• • •

The Hundred Oaks Raiders just beat Winchester, six to five. It was a close call, but Will drove two runs in during the eighth, edging us ahead. I dropped the stats book on the dusty dugout floor and jumped up and down, screaming his name as he rounded first base. He stood on second and took off his batting gloves, grinning over at me.

I really did miss this game.

Now we're packing up our equipment and getting ready to leave.

A bunch of the guys are horsing around over at the concession stand. Sam asks if he can buy out their pizza supply for the bus ride home.

"We only have two pizzas available right now," the worker replies.

"How many slices is that?" Will asks.

"Twenty or so?"

Will consults with Sam. "Maybe we should get Coach to take us to Domino's, dude."

"I hate Domiblows," Sam replies.

"How about Papa John's?" Will asks.

"Gag me with a spoon," Sam jokes.

While they argue, I clear my mind. The sun is blazing. It's not spring yet, but it feels very close, and I love standing here under the blue sky, thinking about how Mom's tulips will bloom soon.

That's when two guys from Winchester approach me.

"Hey," one of them says, checking out my chest.

"Hi," I reply, wishing I had a drink to throw in this guy's face. I look around. Will and Sam are still arguing about pizza, Drew is texting like there's no tomorrow, and Brian is chatting with the Winchester coach.

"Want to hang out?" the Winchester player asks.

"No, thanks," I say, stepping backward.

"C'mon." He gives me a smile that's actually kind of cute. Too bad he already revealed that he's a jerk.

"No."

Out of the corner of my eye, I see Brian coming toward me.

"Fine. Another time," Winchester guy says, and I'm thinking that'll be the end of it, but now Will has seen Brian coming to my "rescue."

"Parker?" Will calls. "You okay?"

Sam begins taking his bat out of his bag (oh my God, he's so ridiculous!) and I'm about to laugh at these guys making a big deal out of nothing. Testosterone is powerful stuff, I chuckle to myself. I love how these guys have become sort of like a family to me.

"Leave her alone!" Paul Briggs shouts at the Winchester players. "She's ours. She's our team mascot!"

Team mascot! Does that mean what I think it means?

Will glances at me as my eyebrows furrow. "All of you on the bus. Now!"

The team rushes toward the parking lot. The two Winchester guys vanish.

Will grabs Paul by the jersey and says, "You owe Parker an apology. And if I ever hear you say something like that again, I'll make sure Coach benches you. Got it?"

"Got it," Paul squeaks out. He must outweigh Will by about a gazillion pounds, but he looks freaked. I've never seen Will Whitfield so pissed. Not even when I won valedictorian over him. When Dr. Salter called us into his office, to tell us the results, a sad knowing smile spread over Will's face. He shook my hand, said congrats, and that was that. Today, fury fills his eyes.

"Sorry," Paul mutters to me before escaping to the bus.

I don't know what to do with my hands. I bite on my pinky nail, chipping the polish, and rock on my heels. Brian's forehead wrinkles as he comes over.

"You all right?" he whispers.

No, I want to say. I feel alone. I thought you were different, but you're not treating me like an adult. Like someone who matters. You're treating me like a plaything. And assholes play both softball and baseball.

My eyes water. "I need to use the bathroom."

Brian squeezes my shoulder and nods. I brush his hand away from me and go into the bathroom to find a toxic warzone. Gross. No way I'm using that. I step back out of the bathroom and see Brian and Will in a hushed conversation, so I decide to eavesdrop on them from around the side of the building. I tiptoe over.

"You showed great leadership today," Brian says to Will. "Taking care of Parker like that. You're a good captain."

"She's a nice girl. She doesn't deserve that."

"What did Paul mean when he called her the team mascot?"

Will pauses. My heart pounds. "Uh, she's hooked up with a couple of guys on the team."

Holy mortification.

"Really?" Brian asks.

"Yeah," Will says quietly.

"But not anymore, right? It wouldn't be good for the team if she's dating a player—"

"She's not dating anyone," Will interrupts. "She told me herself."

Brian hesitates before asking, "Are you into her?"

"Why?"

"I'm your coach. I should know if there could be any potential problems down the line." He's jealous.

"Nah. She's not my type. I'm not interested in a girl like her."

My heart putters to a stop, and a clammy feeling rushes over me and settles in my stomach, hollowing it out.

Will Whitfield couldn't be interested in a girl like me...

Figures.

I turn and sprint back to the bus, my Converses smacking the asphalt. I climb the steps and curl up in my seat. I slip earbuds into my ears, turn on my iPod, and let the *Rent* soundtrack steal my thoughts. Let it erase the hurt. As if it could. My chest heaves in and out. Someone taps my knee. I open my eyes to find Drew slipping into the seat next to me. I pull my earbud out.

"What's wrong?" he whispers.

I turn to stare out the window, hating myself. "Everything's normal."

• • •

Drew invites me over after the game. He makes himself a PB&J. Sitting on a bar stool at the counter, I eat some celery with a bit of peanut butter.

He raps a knife on the counter like he's a woodpecker.

"Why are you so nervous?" I ask, biting into my celery.

"I, um, well..."

"Out with it," I say before swallowing.

"Tate asked me to play mini golf in Nashville tonight."

I squeal. "Really? Did you say yes?"

Drew bites into his sandwich and chews. He takes another bite, and my grin fades as I wait. I dip my celery into the peanut butter.

"You just double dipped your celery into my peanut butter!"

"Stop evading the question," I reply, chewing and double dipping again.

"I said yes," Drew says quietly. He studies his socks. "Please don't tell anybody."

"I won't."

"Especially not Corndog."

"You got it. So you and Tate have been talking...?"

"Mostly messaging on Facebook." He takes another bite of PB&J. "It's good...it's good to know someone like me. It's good to have a friend."

"I'm glad." I can barely sit still I'm so happy for him. "Do you think you're interested in anything more with him?"

Drew's face goes all distorted. "Why are you so interested in what I think of Tate? Is it because of Corndog? Because if I don't like him, you can?"

My chest hurts. My face flushes. "Drew...please..."

"Sorry," he murmurs, opening the fridge and grabbing the milk to pour himself a glass.

I set my celery on my plate and try to ignore the guilt rushing through me. I vow not to tell Drew about baby-sitting with Will tonight, because he'll never believe it's a just-friends thing.

I can have a secret relationship that takes place in a Ford F150 with a guy who's six years older than me, or I can admit my feelings for Will, a boy who's not interested in a girl like me, and lose my best friend in the process.

Or I can be same ole, same ole.

I take a bite of celery sans peanut butter.

• • •

Will opens the front door, and the edges of his mouth slide into a grin. Those blue eyes drop to mine, and he invites me inside the farmhouse that's been in the Whitfield family for something like five generations. "Bo's finishing dinner," he says, taking my jacket to hang it in the closet. "You hungry?"

I wave a hand. "I'm good. Where are your other brothers?"

Will leans against the doorframe. "Rory went to a movie, and Trey's at a friend's house."

"So it's just me, you, and Bo?"

"Yep. Come on." He grabs my hand and leads me to the kitchen, where Bo's playing with his food, dipping chicken nuggets into applesauce.

He scrambles out of his chair and into my arms. I bury my face in his neck, taking in his smell of crayons and juice. Will grins to himself and starts cleaning up Bo's dishes.

"Hey, Bo," he says. "Want to show Parker your birthday party stuff?"

I act surprised. "When's your birthday?"

Bo looks to Will for help.

"You turn five on April Fool's Day, right?" Will says, and his little brother nods. "When Mom called Dad to say she was in labor, he thought she was kidding and was way late to the hospital. I stayed in the delivery room until he rushed in at the last minute."

"That's sweet," I reply, smiling, even though I'm kinda envious of his family.

"My birthday's on April fifth," I tell Bo. "Our birthdays are in the same week."

I leave Will washing dishes and follow Bo to his room, where it looks like his mom has been working on invitations. "You're having a baseball and dinosaur themed party?" He nods, and shows me dinosaur streamers and baseball party favors. Cute.

Bo plops down on the rug to play with Matchbox cars, so I kneel with him and drive a yellow racecar up onto his bed and back to the rug and then up my legs and arms. His mouth forms an O as he watches me.

Will appears in the doorway. "How about a movie?"

"Is that what you want to do?" I ask Bo, who nods. He sure does a lot of nodding. I read online that people with Asperger's usually have repetitive quirks.

Will brings apple slices and cheese, and I carry Bo down the steps to the basement and soon we're watching *School of Rock*, 'cause Bo loves the music. He likes to say "gee-tar" over and over.

Will sits on the cushion right next to me, and Bo wedges himself between us, and after eating his cheese and apple, he promptly falls asleep against Will's side.

"He's adorable," I say, gently mussing Bo's brown curls.

"Thanks," Will replies, focusing on the screen. "I love him."

Bo lets out little snores. "I can see why."

"You're one of the only people he's ever spoken to."

I touch Bo's tiny hand and study his fingers. "That's so sad."

"Mom and Dad are pleased he likes you." Will glances my way. "It's hard for them."

"They've got you and you're great. That's gotta count for a lot."

"You're pretty great yourself," he murmurs, but I pretend not to hear. This afternoon, he told Brian I'm not his type. Would he lie about that? He doesn't know about me and Brian. Could Drew have mentioned something about me and Brian, to keep Will away from me?

No. No way Drew would do that. I want to ask Will what he's thinking, but I can't betray Drew. So we sit here with only a little boy separating us. My life is a twisted pretzel.

"You're going to Vanderbilt, right?" Will asks.

"Yeah."

He chews on a thumb. "Remember how you said on the way to church, how you wished we had been friends before now?"

"I meant it."

"I never did understand why you started ignoring me. I mean, I'm a dork and you're beautiful but you were always so nice—"

"You're not a dork." I take in his blue eyes. "I stopped talking to you because of Laura. She liked you, and I didn't want to get in the way of that."

Will's mouth falls open. "Naw, I know she didn't like me. Not really."

Damn, he's observant. "What school are you going to?" I ask, changing the subject. "Harvard, right?"

He kisses Bo's head. "My great-grandparents started a trust fund for me, before they died, but I'm giving the money to my dad for Bo. So he can go to therapy and a special school."

"What? Can your parents, um, not affo—"

"Things have been hard on the farm lately. Gas and water prices are up and sales have been down…It was a hard winter. I'm going to college somewhere nearby where I can get a full ride instead."

"You're all right, Will Whitfield."

That's when he slides an arm across my shoulders. "I've been giving Vandy serious thought. I'd be close to the farm and my parents and Bo…and you'd be there too."

"Yeah," I say before thinking, glancing at his face, which is focused on me. Holy seriousness. He must've told Brian he's not interested in a girl like me because he doesn't want me to have to stop being manager. "It would be nice having a good friend on campus," I add quickly.

Will's hand is warm on my shoulder. He rubs the side of my neck with his thumb, and it feels so good I shut my eyes and concentrate on not making a sound. And then I'm thinking about how he's a virgin and how I'd love to learn what making love feels like with him, as friends, as partners, with someone who listens to me and cares. We'd do it in our own time.

As soon as the movie ends, I make my excuses and ride my bike home, where I'm alone except for text messages from Brian asking where I am and if he can come over.

The irony. I finally found a boy, Will, a boy I'm willing to risk everything on, to risk breaking my heart, but I stay still. Unmoving.

• • •

Dad studied architecture at UT Knoxville, where Mom played softball.

When he was a boy, he loved poring over floor plans in house catalogs. He still loves reading those magazines today. He wanted to design homes and skyscrapers and bridges, but ended up working in the housing office at Franklin City Hall. And he's fine there, because they pay him pretty decently and he doesn't have to work terribly long hours. He had the opportunity to watch Ryan and me grow up. Mom got to stay home with us instead of having to work.

I remember taking a trip to Asheville, North Carolina, when I was twelve, and Dad was so excited to point out his favorite parts of Biltmore, this huge estate where the Vanderbilts once lived. He loves showing me diagrams of things like the Chrysler Building and the Shanghai Expo. His favorite building ever is the Pantheon in Rome, but he's never been there.

He's never been there because he saves all his money. He doesn't want Ryan to work while he's in college. He doesn't want me to either. Dad's made a lot of sacrifices for me and my brother.

If there's one thing I want, God, it's for Dad to take a trip to Italy. I want him to explore the Vatican and see the sculptures at the Medici Chapel in Florence. I want him to study the Bridge of Sighs in Venice.

I want so much for my father, Lord, because he wants so much for me.

Written while tucked under my covers on March 7. Burned.

• • •

When I don't answer his texts, Brian calls my cell.

"Can we get together?" he asks, sounding upset. I can hear a hockey game in the background. Maybe he's watching the Predators on TV?

"I'm sick of being in your truck."

"Yeah?"

I whisper, "I deserve more than that."

He hesitates for a long time. "I want more, but I don't know what I can give you right now."

Will, Will, Will. I want him. Just thinking of him makes my skin tingle, and I keep reliving that afternoon we spent napping in my bed. Wondering what might've happened if we'd kissed. I doubt we'd be close like we are now. It's like relaxing during a long snow when the streets are so covered with ice, school closes. Things with Will have been sorta delayed. I've gotten a chance to settle in, to get to know him for him, and him for me.

Wild to think that, a couple of weeks ago, I wanted Brian bad. And I'm not sure I do anymore. Admitting this, I feel stress pulsing through me. And it's not only because of Will that I'm thinking this way. It doesn't feel right.

"Maybe we should be friends?" I ask Brian, my voice shaking like crazy.

"Come on, Park," he murmurs. "We've got something."

"But…"

"Yeah?"

I summon some courage. "I want you to listen to me when I talk. I want to do something other than sit in your truck. Am I even your girlfriend?"

He clears his throat. I listen to the hockey game in the background. "You know I like you and want you, but we can't date for real."

"Okay, well I guess that's it then. I'll see you at practice Monday," I say, and as Brian tries to interrupt, I quickly add, "Bye" and hang up.

I'm proud of myself for doing that.

Aaron Pritchard and Matt Higgins and other guys had a thing for me, but I treated their feelings like they didn't matter, believing that guys don't mind one-night flings. I thought I liked Brian seriously. But the way he's treating me sucks. Shame fills my heart, when I think of the guys I used to prove that I'm not like Mom.

• • •

On Sunday evening, Drew lets himself in the front door, carrying a bowl of popcorn and the *Half-Blood Prince* DVD. We decided to have a Harry Potter movie night at my house, because his mom recently started dating this guy, Otto.

Otto always wants to play dominoes. Drew and I have nothing against dominoes, but Otto takes the game very seriously and rolls his eyes when we start building fortresses and then knock them down with a catapult made out of a spoon and a salt shaker.

We curl up on the couch, and he lets me lean against him. Television light brightens the dim room.

"Ginny Weasley sure grew up to be a saucy minx, eh?" Drew asks, shoving a handful of popcorn in his mouth.

I'm grinning. "So did Neville Longbottom."

"You think Neville Longbottom is a saucy minx?"

"No, no. He grew up to be kinda cute. So did Ron."

"Don't you think Draco is hot in an evil way?"

"No way," I say, shoving Drew with an elbow. "He must spend hours a day gelling his hair. I could never date a guy who spends so much time on his appearance."

"I bet Coach Hoffman spends a lot of time on his hair. It always looks perfect, even if he's been wearing a cap."

"We're not dating."

Drew turns to look at me, giving me a hard stare that says he doesn't believe me.

"It's true," I say quietly. "I asked if I was his girlfriend and he said we can't date for real. I guess he only wants to fool around."

"Is that what you want?"

"Not really." What I want is a two-way relationship. "I hung up on him last night after I basically said I'm not hooking up again until he lets me have a say in what we do."

"Good for you."

"But it sucks because I thought he really liked me."

Drew pauses the movie. "Some guys are straight-up jerks. You can't do anything about that."

"He's not a total jerk…" He's confused and down and wants to stay young. Nothing wrong with that, but I wish he would consider my feelings more.

Drew puts an arm around me and whispers, "Did you do it with him?"

I shake my head. "He said he wanted to when I turn eighteen. But I'm not ready for that. With anybody."

"I wish I'd waited…To have sex, I mean."

"You regret doing it with Amy?"

He hesitates. "I love her. But I want to sleep with someone I'm *in* love with."

"How was mini golf?" I've been dying to know how Drew's date thing went last night. I couldn't get any details out of Tate this morning at church.

He stuffs a handful of popcorn into his mouth. He smiles a little. "It was good. I won by a landslide. I have no idea why someone so not athletic would want to play mini golf."

I snorggle. "Maybe that's why he wouldn't give me any details."

Drew glances at me sideways. "He didn't mention me?"

I get the feeling that, if not for Drew, Tate never would've said anything to me about himself, about his life. He seems kinda private. "He didn't say anything. But he smiled when I brought you up. Are you going to see him again?" I'm excited for my friend.

"We want to get to know each other." He blushes. "I haven't even told Mom about me yet…Hey, listen. Corndog looked at my article about if the Braves should make a trade for a new bat in the middle of the order. He said he loved it, but gave me some edits. Can you read it to see if you have ideas on how to make it stronger?"

"Yeah, no prob—"

The front door opens, and Dad walks in. He says hello to us and pats my head softly.

"Were you out with Veena?" I ask, turning to hang over the back of the couch.

"She's hot," Drew says, chomping on popcorn. "I saw her out the window when she came over to your place last weekend."

Dad's face turns pink. "I don't think we're going to see each other again." He says it matter-of-factly and makes his way toward the kitchen. Drew and I exchange looks.

I leap to my feet and follow Dad. "What? Why? Did you have a fight?"

He opens the fridge. Bright white light tumbles out. "Jack Taylor mentioned his wife is concerned about my relationship with Veena."

"So?" Mrs. Taylor used to be Mom's friend; you can guess how that turned out.

Dad stares inside the refrigerator. "She and Jack don't think I should be off dating a younger woman when I should be taking care of you and your brother."

"What? We don't care. We like Veena!"

"That's not the point. This isn't the right time for me to try dating again." He sighs heavily, and rubs his eyes with a finger and thumb. He can't really believe that!

"We want you to be happy!"

He pulls out the orange juice. "It doesn't matter what I want."

"That is such bullshit," I exclaim.

"Watch your mouth."

Ryan appears in the doorway, wearing jeans and a T-shirt. He got a haircut yesterday and now looks a lot more like he did pre-Vanderbilt. I can't help smiling.

"What are you arguing about?" he asks.

"Dad broke it off with Veena," I reply slowly.

My brother is silent, but sadness takes over his face. He turns and leaves the kitchen. His bedroom door shuts.

I close my eyes, lean my head against the wall and pray to God, to anyone who might be listening, to please help me. Please help my family. Hasn't our church taken enough from us?

And now they have to take our new happiness too?

Why?

Why is Dad letting these people factor into his happiness so much? Why do we care? We can't control what those assholes say, but we can ignore them. If we were to just forget them and focus on God, would everything be better?

i'm not that kind of girl
28 days until i turn 18

After Monday's practice, I'm unlocking my bike when Brian comes jogging up. He flips his hat around backward. His cutoff sweatshirt sleeves hang lazily over his elbows.

"Hey," he says, breathlessly.

"What's up?" I try to hide how annoyed I am.

"Want to do something tonight?" His eyes dart around.

Does he want to do dinner at Foothills? Or go to the Little Duck River again with Brandy? "You want to do something with me?"

"I do. Can I drop by at around eleven?" He gives me a sexy grin, a grin making it obvious what he wants. Which is not what I want.

I glance around the parking lot. Will and Drew are standing next to Drew's VW bug, staring over at me. "I'll text you later."

"Is that a no?" he asks.

I play with the hem of my sweater. "I can't."

Brian reaches into his back pocket for a new piece of gum. "Call me whenever you're ready to hang out, I guess. See you tomorrow."

I hop on my bike and pedal home, pissed at myself for letting him go down my pants. And to think I thought we had a real connection.

We have a physical attraction, and friendship, and commonalities, but there's no romance. I want romance so much.

At my house, I lock my bike in the garage, then drag myself inside, all the while wishing the sweet and funny Brian I knew a few weeks ago would come back. I'm on my way to my room when I notice a leg sticking out of the bathroom. Ryan's leg. I rush forward to find him sprawled out on the tiles, an empty bottle of Robitussin in his fist.

"Shit! Ryan!" I yell, dropping to his side. I check for a pulse and listen for breathing. He's got both. I pull my cell phone out of my pocket and I'm just about to call an ambulance when he lets out a moan.

He smacks his lips, and his eyes flicker open. His gaze meets mine.

"Are you okay?" I blurt. Tears drip down my face.

"Ugghhh."

"Why?" I cry, plucking the bottle from his hand and throwing it in the trash. "Why do you keep doing this?"

"Sorry," he moans.

I grab a washcloth from the closet, wet it, and begin dabbing at his forehead and neck. I'm wondering if I should call Daddy Denial to ask if I should take Ryan to the hospital when the doorbell rings.

"I'll be right back," I tell Ryan. "Don't move, got it?"

He shuts his eyes and keeps cleaning his face with the washcloth. I quickly check my appearance in the mirror—I've got red, puffy eyes.

I peer through the peephole. Will's here, still in his jersey and baseball pants. He adjusts his cap. I pull open the door. "Hey."

"Hi," he replies, focusing on his cleats. "Can we talk? I dropped by because—"

"Can we talk later?" I rush to ask.

His head pops up. "What's wrong?" He watches me wipe tears away. The smells of fabric softener and fried chicken threaten to make me sick.

He steps forward and wraps me in a hug. "Talk to me."

The story tumbles out of my mouth. Will releases me and charges through the front door, with me on his heels. He finds Ryan and kneels down next to him. Will does the same thing I did: checks his pulse and listens to his breathing.

"Let's take him to the hospital."

"Are you sure?" I whisper.

"I'm fine," Ryan slurs.

"I have never been so sure of anything," Will says, finding my eyes. "We're taking him in."

• • •

At the hospital, we're not allowed in the emergency room. Will paces around the waiting room while I pick at my orange nail polish.

Dad was on his way home from work when I called. He's rushing over to the hospital now.

"Can you please sit with me?" I ask Will. "You're making me nervous."

He gives me a slight smile and slides in next to me. Our hips touch, and he leans over and wraps his hands behind his neck. Nurses and orderlies zip back and forth in front of us. The paging system calls for Dr. Turner to report straight to the ICU. A woman with a broken leg rolls by in a wheelchair.

"Thank you for bringing us," I tell Will quietly. "An ambulance would've cost too much, and I don't drive often." I clutch my knees.

"Does this happen a lot? With your brother?" he asks.

"He's always high, if that's what you mean."

"Has he ever ODed before?"

I shake my head. "Not that I know of. I can't believe this."

"Bad things happen sometimes."

"Yeah."

It's cool that Will is here supporting me, and not judging. If anyone from Forrest Sanctuary finds out about this, I can't imagine the grief the church will give my family. A few years ago, Tasha Reed drank too much at a field party and had to be rushed to the hospital, and everyone at church had a field day with that one for ages.

An orderly walks by pushing some medical contraption covered by cords. That's when I see Veena over by the nurse's station. She spots me. Her eyes narrow, and she tightens her ponytail, starting toward me. Her pink scrubs bring out her tan skin and brown curls, and I can't believe Dad would be so stupid as to let our church convince him to give her up.

"What are you doing here?" Veena asks, as Will and I stand to greet her.

"Her brother's in the ER. We just brought him in," Will replies, and Veena's gone, running toward a set of double doors before I even get to say hello.

Will helps me to sit back down and this time, he puts an arm around me and talks about how Bo was in the hospital a lot when he was little. "One time last year, he had pneumonia. Dad was in the room with him and he accidentally fell asleep. I guess Bo saw someone walking by with a bag of Doritos, so he ripped the IV out of his leg, climbed out of the hospital bed and ran down the hall after the chips."

I laugh softly and smile over at him. "All you Whitfield boys are such trouble."

"Proud of it."

That's when Dad comes rushing into the ER and lifts me into his arms. Then he sets me down and beelines for the nurse's station. I ask them to page Veena, and sadness and confusion and hurt cloud Dad's face when she appears from behind those ominous double doors.

"How's my son?" he hurries to ask her.

"He'll be fine," Veena tells Dad, placing a hand on his arm, to calm him. "We pumped his stomach, but there's no irreparable damage."

Veins bulge in Dad's throat. "Thank you," he tells her. "For taking care of him." Then Dad wraps a hand around the back of my neck and kisses the top of my head. "I love you."

"I love you too," I reply. Veena averts her gaze, dabbing at her eye with a thumb.

"Dr. Matlock wants to keep Ryan overnight for observation," Veena says.

"Should I call your mom?" Will asks me, touching my elbow.

"No," Dad and I say at the same time. I don't think either of us can take that right now. It seems like he just noticed Will is here with me, because his back goes rigid and he briefly shakes Will's hand, avoiding his eyes.

Dad's going to stay overnight with Ryan, so Will says he'll give me a ride home. Dad eyes Will, his face suspicious. "You go straight home, and no visitors tonight, okay?"

"Okay," I reply.

Will puts an arm around me, and as we're walking to the parking lot, Veena hurries after us. Her pink scrubs glow under the parking lot lights. She wraps her arms around herself to keep warm. "Parker, can I talk to you for a minute?"

Will gently touches my lower back before moving away.

Veena glances at him. "He's cute, huh?"

I pinch my lip and nod.

"Are you dating him?"

"No. He's just a friend."

She gives me a look. Nothing gets past her. "I'm glad you're hanging out with someone your age, at least."

"Sorry about what happened with Dad," I say, changing the subject.

She shakes her head and laughs to herself. She seems resigned. "The people around here don't make it easy to fit in, that's for sure."

"You're telling me."

She places a hand on my upper arm. "But are you all right? Do you need to talk? About anything?"

I don't think I am okay, no. "Everything's cool," I tell her.

"Okay, well maybe I'll see you around sometime."

"I'll be at church on Sunday."

She smiles sadly. "I don't think I'm going back to Forrest Sanctuary. But I get coffee all the time at the 41 Drive-In."

"You should look up Will's church. It's called Westwood. They're very nice there." Veena smiles and thanks me, and says she needs to get back inside. "Thanks for everything," I add, wishing so bad that she and Dad had worked out, and then I'm buckled into Will's truck and we're heading back to my house in silence. Streetlights whiz by. I watch his dangling pine tree air freshener swing back and forth.

At home, he jingles his keys as he walks me to the door. We stand under the porch light as gnats buzz around our heads.

"Thanks again," I whisper, bowing my head. He puts two fingers under my chin, lifting it to where we can see each other.

"I'll see you tomorrow," he replies, pulling me into a hug. I dry my eyes on his sweatshirt and he responds by giving me a quick kiss on the top of my head.

"Night," I say, touching the patch of hair his lips just touched. My heart beats like crazy. "Wait. Can you come in for a minute?"

Without a word, he follows me inside and to my bedroom. The streetlamp outside my window cuts a beam of light across the rug. He stares down at me for a long time, like I'm the only thing in the universe.

"I'd better go home," he says, clutching the side of his neck.

"Yeah, you should go." I'm praying that Drew doesn't notice Will's truck in the driveway. But mostly I'm praying Will doesn't try to kiss me tonight, *and* fearing that he won't.

"I'll stay until you're tucked in," he says, so I put on my pajamas while he waits in the hallway, then I let him back into my room.

"Wait. Why'd you drop by again?" I ask.

He smiles and shakes his head. "It's not important tonight." He takes my hand, leading me toward my bed. I crawl under the covers and he pulls them up to my neck.

"I'm glad you were here."

"Me too," he says, sitting on my bed. He runs a hand over my head. His eyes bore into mine. He leans over and presses a kiss to my forehead, says good night, and leaves my room, looking back at me one last time.

It would've been so easy to invite him into my bed.

But I don't want to be that kind of girl.

I miss the girl I used to be.

falling to pieces
25 days until i turn 18

"Let's bring it in, guys!" Brian shouts to the team.

Thursday's practice just ended, so I dump ice out of two coolers onto the ground and lug them to the left field equipment shed, where I store them on a shelf. This is one of the first moments I've had to myself in days, so I lean against the wall, inhaling the musky scent of worn leather. A fly buzzes past me. I dip my thumbs into my jeans pockets and shut my eyes.

This week has been too emotional. Too confusing. Ryan stayed in the hospital overnight and came home on Tuesday, but when I asked Dad if we're going to get him some help, Dad said he's not ready to make any decisions yet.

I checked our insurance. It doesn't cover counseling, or I'd get him an appointment myself. Maybe Vanderbilt has some free services for students?

I suck in a breath, listening to the laughter coming from outside the shed. I'm enjoying the peace when I hear a voice.

"Hey."

I twirl around to find Will standing in the doorway, the sun filling the air around his body with bright white light.

"Hey." I give him a grin.

"Can we talk?" he asks. "I want to tell you why I dropped by the other night."

"Sure. What's up?"

His mouth twitches and he rubs his palms together. "I was wondering if you'd go to prom with me."

A big smile leaps across my face, but then I remember. Drew. I shouldn't. But I want this. I face the wooden wall. Catch my breath. "I'd really love that…"

"Okay, so we're on?" He sounds excited.

"I, um." I toe the basket of balls at my feet. "Before I can answer, I need to figure a few things out."

"Oh." I turn to find him furrowing his eyebrows. He's so sweet.

"It's nothing to do with you," I say, even though it is.

He takes his cap off, stuffs it in his back pocket and steps toward me. "Do you really want to go with me?"

"Yes," I whisper, and swallow. I find his eyes. He takes a step closer. I take a step closer.

"So let's go together."

I glance at his lips, he smiles down at me and goose bumps pop all over my arms, telling me this is right, but it's wrong. The smell of apple wafts under my nose. His shampoo?

"I'm, uh," he says. "I've enjoyed getting to know you better and…I want to try for something more."

"With me?"

He nods. "I wasn't sure at first, you know, if I wanted to pursue something serious with you." He moves a step closer—so close his breath warms my cheek. "But I do."

"You do?" I ask softly.

His hand slides onto my hip. "Yeah."

It's what I've wanted. A relationship with a guy I can trust. A good friend. An equal. He makes my heart slam against my chest. I've never wanted to kiss someone this much in my life. His other hand settles on my waist and I slide my fingers inside his loose sweatshirt sleeves, making him tremble. Our chests press together; I can feel his pulse.

Will leans in toward my lips, his hair flopping against my nose, and I want this to happen but it can't. I step back, and he stumbles forward.

"I can't do this until I talk to Drew."

He rights himself, looking embarrassed, then confused. "Bates?"

"Yeah."

He scratches his nose. "Whatever you need...but you're not messing with me, right? I wouldn't be a one-night thing?"

"No no no." I shake my head and look him straight in the eye.

"I would've asked you out a long time ago, but I wanted to make sure we could have something real." His voice stumbles.

"I want something real too, but I need to do some stuff first, okay? Trust me?"

Will slides a hand onto my shoulder. "I can wait."

"Thanks." I slip my hand on top of his and squeeze. He begins to lean his forehead toward mine when I hear a loud cough.

I jerk away from Will to find Brian standing in the doorway, pursing his lips. He secures his bat under an arm.

"You told me you weren't interested in her, Whitfield," Brian says. God, he looks so pissed.

"Nothing's going on," Will says quickly.

"Not sure I believe you, but anyway, I don't think this is the time or place for this, okay?" He points from me to Will.

"Okay, Coach," Will says.

"Coach Burns told Parker that she isn't allowed to date players and still be a manager," Brian replies. "You're excused, Whitfield."

"But—"

"You're excused."

Will glances at me, then walks out of the equipment shed. My heart pounds while Brian glares at me. He glances over his shoulder and shuts the shed door. "What's going on, Park?" he whispers, setting his bat against the wall.

"Will asked me to prom." I wring my hands and bite my lip.

"What did you say?" Brian asks softly, moving toward me.

"No. I said no. For now."

"For now?"

"I said I'd think about it."

He lets out a mean laugh and shakes his head. "God, I'm so stupid."

"Why?"

"Getting involved with someone your age. I should've known you'd never be mature enough—"

"I've been trying to talk to you about what I want and what I need, and you never listen—"

"Because nothing's at stake for you! My whole life is on the line here, Parker. For you! Because I like you—"

"If you really liked me, you'd listen—"

"If you really liked me, you wouldn't be cheating on me in the equipment shed with a guy named Corndog and—"

"I didn't even know we're in a relationship. You said we can't date for real, and I don't know what we are—"

"We're nothing."

I bow my head and try to swallow the lump in my throat. Doesn't work. I cough. I liked Brian. Things started off so well. He seems just as confused as I am.

"Nothing's happened with Will." I don't even know why I'm telling Brian this. It's none of his business. But I guess I want to show I can be a good person. A tear drips down my cheek. I wipe it away with the heel of my hand.

Brian gives me a look of sympathy and comes closer. He brushes my hair off my shoulder and leaves his hand there. "I'm sorry I yelled at you," he whispers.

His mouth hovers next to my ear and I'm thinking he'll kiss it, and I'm about to tell him that I don't want this right now, that we rushed into this-whatever-it-is and we should get out while we can, before we both get hurt more or get in trouble or he really falls hard, like I'm falling hard for Will, when the shed door opens.

"Ohmigod!" Laura blurts, and slaps a hand over her mouth.

I step away from Brian. Try to get my breathing under control. I clutch my chest, staring my former best friend down. She turns and flies across the field.

Holy hell. What's she gonna do?

• • •

I'm summoned to the principal's office at 8:16 on Friday morning. I'm surprised it took that long.

Last night, Brian and I spoke briefly on the phone.

"Maybe you should call Laura," he said. "Tell her that she misunderstood what she saw."

I chipped all the soft pink polish off my nails. I couldn't stop shaking. "She hates me, Brian."

"So what are we gonna do then?"

"Pretend like nothing happened? If I call her up, it's as good as admitting guilt."

"But if Dr. Salter starts asking around, Bates might say something."

"He won't say anything. He's my best friend."

"And you're sure Whitfield doesn't know anything about me and you?"

"Do you really think he would've invited me to prom if he knew about you?"

Brian went silent for a minute. "I would've taken you to prom, if we had been in high school at the same time."

"I probably would've said no."

He laughed softly. "Why's that?"

"You're a perv! You chiseled through the concrete between the locker rooms and spied on girls!"

"I bet I could've gotten you to say yes."

I smiled at my ceiling, liking that Brian and I were talking normally again. Everything got messed up the minute we started kissing. "Okay, maybe I would've said yes."

"I bet you'd look really beautiful in a gown."

"Thanks," I whispered.

"Listen, I'll see you tomorrow, okay?"

We hung up, and I curled under the covers. My phone buzzed. Mom texted: Good night. I love you.

Now I'm thinking of her as I walk to the principal's office. When I was a little girl, I would tug on her skirts and dresses, to get her to smile down at me. I loved seeing her face. Friendly, tan, smooth, beautiful, loving. I wish I could see her now. I wish she had stayed with us. None of this ever would've happened if Mom were here. She would've noticed me sneaking out of the house late at night.

She would've spotted the small bruise on my collarbone where Brian kissed me too hard. She would've noticed the condoms in my purse, the ones I bought just in case.

She'd know, plain and simple.

But she's gone, and I need to face that. Just like I'm about to face the principal. His secretary doesn't meet my eyes as she tells me to go on in, where I find my father and Dr. Salter chatting about graduation.

"Hey, Dad," I say, accepting a kiss on the cheek before plopping down in the seat beside him. "What are you doing here?"

"Dr. Salter called and asked me to drop by before work. Is everything okay?" The circles under his eyes have gotten worse since he decided not to pursue Veena. Since Ryan went to the hospital.

"I hope so," I reply, squeezing my knees.

Dad and I turn our attention to the principal, who stares me down. He studies my face and my hands start trembling, but I will them to stop. I can't show any guilt. None.

"What's going on?" Dad says.

Dr. Salter asks, "Parker, are you involved with Coach Hoffman?"

"What?" Dad exclaims, sitting up straight.

I lie, choosing my words carefully. "We talk sometimes, sure."

"That's what he said too," Dr. Salter says. "But are you sure nothing ever happened with him? Romantically or otherwise?"

I let my mouth fall open. "No, sir."

"What's Dr. Salter talking about?" Dad asks, resting a hand on my back. "I thought you were dating that Corn Fritter fellow."

"It's Corndog, Dad. Not Corn Fritter."

"You're dating Will Whitfield?" Dr. Salter asks, picking up a glass paperweight. "I wasn't aware."

"Why would you be interested in that?" I ask.

The principal plays with the paperweight. "It'll be a nice human interest addition to the piece I'm writing about our valedictorian and salutatorian for the *Franklin Times*. But Laura Martin's allegations are quite serious. She claims she found you with Coach Hoffman in the equipment shed. She said he was kissing your ear."

"No," I blurt, shifting in my seat.

Dad's eyes bulge. "That's impossible."

"Laura hates me," I say. "She'll lie about anything to make me feel bad—"

Dr. Salter holds up a hand. "I should have already turned this over to the school board for a proper investigation, but you're such a good student, and you've never been in trouble. And I'd hate to ruin Coach Hoffman's career before it even starts." The principal coughs and averts his eyes, to concentrate on his inspirational calendar, which reads CONFIDENCE.

"There must be some mistake," Dad says. "Laura couldn't have seen my daughter with Coach Hoffman. Parker is a good Christian girl, and she's dating a good Christian boy. He goes to Westwood, and we go to Forrest Sanctuary." Dad's face is red and his neck bulges.

I squeeze my hands between my knees and stare down. I can't believe I did this. Dad's lying for me, and he doesn't even know it. And now he's dragging poor Will into this. Please let this be enough for Dr. Salter. Please let it be enough. I promise you, Lord, I'll never do anything wrong again if you can help me out of this.

I can't ruin Brian's life. I can't.

"Call Corndog down here," Dad insists. "He'll tell you the truth."

"Dad, don't."

"Why not?" Dr. Salter asks.

I pause. "My friend likes Will, so we're keeping it a secret."

"Which friend?"

"I can't say. It's not my place to tell."

Dr. Salter uses his intercom. "Marti, please summon Will Whitfield to my office."

I shut my eyes and wish Mom was here. We sit in silence for three minutes until Will comes rushing in the door. He slows down when he sees me, and drops into the chair next to mine.

"Hello, Dr. Salter. Mr. Shelton." Will nods at them, then lays a hand on my arm. "You okay?" he whispers.

I nod slowly, relieved that he's playing the part he doesn't know he's cast in. I hate myself for this. Hate. Tears prick my eyes. I sniffle. Then I put pressure on Will's foot, giving him the only message I can. Help.

The principal starts, "Will, I'm sorry to bring you out of class like this—"

"Tell Dr. Salter the truth," Dad says. "That you're dating my daughter. Or maybe even doing more with her. I did catch you in her bed that day."

My chin bobs against my chest, and I let out a low cry. Poor Will. He doesn't deserve this.

"We're not sleeping together. No, sir," Will says quietly. His face turns the pinkest pink.

I step on his foot harder.

"But yeah, we're dating," Will says, looking from me to the principal.

"And you're keeping it a secret?" Dr. Salter asks, rapping the paper-weight against his desk. Jesus. The man should forget educating kids and become a detective.

Will glances at me. "Yes, sir. For a friend's sake."

"Really?"

"A mutual friend is interested in me," Will says, then hesitates. "But it'll never work out. We don't want my friend to know yet."

He didn't say he or she. Will is a perceptive guy.

"Well, your story matches Coach Hoffman's," Dr. Salter says to me. I pull a deep breath through my nose.

"What story?" Will asks, leaning forward.

"Laura Martin claimed she saw Coach Hoffman and Miss Shelton interacting in an inappropriate manner in the baseball equipment shed yesterday afternoon."

"The equipment shed?" Will blurts. His voice squeaks.

"Yes…" Dr. Salter says, and Will laughs harshly. "What's so funny?"

Will grabs my hand and kisses my knuckles. "Coach Hoffman caught us in the equipment shed yesterday, and then he told me I was acting inappropriately and asked me to leave. Did Laura see you when Coach Hoffman was lecturing you?" Will asks me. His blue eyes are hard. Angry.

"Um, yeah."

"You were in the equipment shed with Corn Fritter?" Dad asks me.

"Corndog," Will, Dr. Salter, and I say simultaneously.

"I think we're through here for now," the principal announces, standing to shake hands with Dad. "Miss Shelton? Can I talk to you and Coach Hoffman about your baseball managing duties?"

"Yes, sir," I say, watching Dad and Will file out.

The principal comes out from around his desk. He avoids my gaze and opens his side door to reveal Brian sitting in an armchair, rapping his foot on the floor. He stands and makes his way into Dr. Salter's office. We sit back down.

"Hi, Coach Hoffman," I say softly.

"Hey, Parker."

The principal runs a hand over his head, then sits behind his desk. He raps his paperweight. "I said your stories add up, but I'm afraid I still need to present this to the school board. I'm required to report any accusations against active faculty."

"Sir—" Brian starts, looking freaked out.

"But Laura hates me," I interrupt.

Dr. Salter looks at Brian. "If you did nothing wrong, you have nothing to worry about. They won't find any evidence…right?"

"Evidence?" I ask quietly.

"If the board does an investigation, will they find evidence that you and Coach Hoffman have spoken outside of school activities?" Dr. Salter's eyes bore into mine. "Have you talked on the phone? Over the Internet? Have you ever gone anywhere together?" He pauses. "If you're telling me they'll find nothing, we'll remove the accusation from the coach's file. But if there is any reason they might believe something is going on between you two—"

"Sir," Brian says, pinching the bridge of his nose. "What can I do to make this stop right here? I'll do anything."

My eyes are watering. I sniffle. "I'll give up being valedictorian."

Brian shakes his head. "You don't have to do that."

The principal looks from me to Brian, and I know he knows the truth. "Coach, if you resign today, we'll consider this matter closed."

Brian doesn't hesitate. "Done."

• • •

We go into the hallway, where I clutch Dad's elbow. My teeth are chattering. Will's hanging his head, and I think he might cry.

"I'm sorry for the mess," Dad says, shaking Brian's hand. "I know your parents go to Forrest Sanctuary and that no son of theirs would ever do something wrong like this. My sincerest apologies."

"Uh, yes, sir." Brian releases Dad's hand. Pain covers Brian's face. "I'm sorry if this misunderstanding embarrassed you and your family, Mr. Shelton." He heads down the hallway toward his office.

By resigning, Brian basically admitted guilt just now, and if and when people hear the rumors, I bet my family will be more embarrassed than ever.

Dad cups my neck with a hand. "I'm sure your being caught in the equipment shed with Corndog was a one-time occurrence. Right, Parker?"

"Yes, Dad."

"Definitely. A one-time occurrence," Will mutters, rubbing his eyes.

"We'll pray about this and your brother later." Dad shakes his head at me, gives Will a dirty look, and ducks into the bathroom across the hall.

Gee, thanks for the support, Dad. I press a palm to the trophy case and wipe a tear from my face. Brian's resigning. Because of me. Jobs are hard to come by these days, and I ruined a good opportunity for him. And I lied. I sinned. I'm a terrible person. I miss Mom.

God, where are you? I'm sorry I keep doing these things. Can't you help me be a good person? Please.

Will's still standing next to me, silent.

"Thank you," I whisper.

"Why won't you go to prom with me? The truth this time, please."

"I didn't say no. I need to take care of some things, I told you that."

He stares at me sideways. "What are these things?" His voice is rough.

"I need to talk to Drew."

"And?"

Tears are rolling down my face, and I don't know what hurts worse: my heart, or that Will isn't rushing to comfort me. He inches away from me, folding his arms.

"Is it true?" he asks. "What the principal said? About you and Coach Hoffman?"

I look over my shoulder, to make sure no one's listening. Tears blur my vision. I don't say anything. That should be enough of an answer for Will, the smartest guy I know.

"I thought you were someone else," he says. "I came to the conclusion that you weren't who I thought you were—a girl who gets around with every guy she sees. I thought I had it all wrong. But I guess I was right the first time. You messed with my friends. I don't know why I was so damned stupid to think I'd be different—"

"But you are different—"

"Don't." Will shakes his head. "I'm just glad I never kissed you. Or worse, lost it to you. What a waste that would've been, huh?"

I lean against the trophy case. Tears soak my shirt. I feel my makeup melting off. "A waste?" I whisper. I never wanted this for me.

And worse, I threw Will under the bus. For nothing. Brian had to resign anyway.

The bell rings, and students start moving through the halls. Will stays next to me but says nothing. People are pointing at me. That's when Drew comes rushing up. "What'd you do to her, man?" he asks Will. My best friend pulls me into his arms. I rest my chin on his shoulder. Will slams the glass door open and stalks toward the parking lot.

Dad exits the bathroom. "Parker," he says quietly. "I love you and care about you, but I don't want to be called away from work again because you got caught in the equipment shed with Corndog. Understand?"

"What?" Drew whispers. "You what?"

"Yes, Dad," I say, sniffling, and he leaves, not looking back at me.

Drew's face falls. "You lied to me? You're really fooling around with him?"

"Corndog only pretended that," I exclaim. "To cover for me. With Brian." I move to fall back into Drew's arms, but he scoots away from me. "We've never hooked up or kissed or anything."

"You were messing around with both of them? Did you use Corndog to cover up who you're really interested in?"

"No, no." I reach for him again, but he steps backward. "Will lied. To help me. To help Brian."

"I can't believe you," he whispers. "I stuck by you. Through everything. All your mood swings and cutting out the world. I told people you weren't a freak. I told them you were shy and cared about school."

"Drew—"

"And I told you my secret," he whispers. "And then you took it from me." His big brown eyes go glossy.

"Drew, that's not what happened. Can you list—"

"Everything with you is such bullshit. You probably got Tate to talk to me so you could have Will all to yourself. Right?"

I tried to be a good friend…And now he won't even listen. I had a chance with Will. I turned down a date to prom. A real date with a real guy who truly wanted me. All for a friend who won't even hear me out.

I don't have anything.

"I'll see you later, then," I whisper, and decide to skip school today. I leave to go home.

Wherever that is.

I run into Laura, Allie, and Mel on the way to the bike rack. They start whispering. So I start shouting.

"Thanks for turning me into Dr. Salter, Laura. I'll pray for you. Lord knows you'd never do it for me because you're so jealous. Judge thy neighbor, eh?"

They shut up and stare at me. I've never said anything like that before. And you know what? I didn't get struck by lightning. I don't even feel guilty.

I tell my eyes to stop crying. Fat chance of that.

alternative spring break

"Don't call me again."

Will hung up on me.

When I called Drew, he sounded like he was choking on his tears. "I can't talk to you right now. I really can't. Bye."

When I called Brian, no answer.

He quit his job. Because of something I basically forced him into, something I was ready to give up the moment I had feelings for Will. Brian's right. I am immature. I try calling his cell, but he doesn't pick up. He's not on Skype, and he defriended me on Facebook! And after a couple of hours, he doesn't return any of my emails. It's after 6:00 p.m., so I open the church directory I stole and find his parents' address. I Google map directions, and I'm on my bike and pedaling down the road in less than a minute.

At his house, I locate the stairs leading to the apartment above the garage, then lean my bike against a tree. I wipe my sweaty palms on my jeans, take a quick look around the neighborhood to make sure no one sees me, then quietly climb the steps. I knock and knock and knock. I knock until my knuckles feel raw.

"He's not here," a man calls out from down below. I recognize him from the Forrest Sanctuary church directory. Mr. Hoffman.

"When will he be back?" I ask.

The man lifts both shoulders. "He went to Birmingham to visit a friend. I'm not sure when he plans to come back. He said he quit his job over at the high school. Any idea why?"

He left without saying good-bye? Without checking to make sure I was okay?

I'm nobody.

My mom left me.

My dad thinks I'm a big fat sinner.

My brother is on another plane of existence.

Drew's angry with me.

Will...

Nothing. I'm nothing.

"You go to Forrest Sanctuary, right?" Mr. Hoffman asks, narrowing his eyes at me. "David Shelton's daughter?"

"Yes, sir." My hands shake.

"Can I give Brian a message?"

"No message."

I turn and make my way down the steps and climb on my bike before anyone else sees I'm here. I pedal home, where I find Ryan curled up in a ball on the living room couch.

"Hi," I say to him.

"Yo." He rests his head on a cushion, not bothering to ask about my face. My tears.

Dad's sitting in his armchair, reading the Bible. He looks up at me and shakes his head, then goes back to reading. Bags hang under his eyes.

"I wish you hadn't given up on Veena so quickly," I tell Dad.

He jerks his head up and finds my eyes. "What happened with Veena is none of your business. I prayed about it."

"Prayer doesn't solve everything, Dad. It's not going to solve Ryan's problems. Or mine. You had a good thing with Veena, but you're so damned stubborn, and you have to listen to everything the people at church say. You only gave up because they told you to. I'm sorry you'll keep on being lonely like this."

Dad takes off his glasses and runs a hand over his Bible.

I focus on my brother. "And Ryan? I'm feeling shitty. Thanks for asking. And no, I'm not making you dinner tonight. Make it your damned self."

He doesn't open his eyes.

I stalk down the hall to my room, and without bothering to put on pajamas, I crawl under my covers and cry, cry, cry. Brian quit his job. Because of me. I might drown in the guilt. Neither Dad nor Ryan knocks on the door. I don't get any texts. Drew doesn't come over to read *Cosmo* with me. Will doesn't show up by way of a lawnmower.

"Please, God," I whisper. "Please. Tell me what to do. Please." I clear my head of all thoughts. I imagine how good it feels to swing at a pitch. To connect. To send a line drive over the second baseman's head.

God, please.

My cell beeps. I jump. Look at the text from Mom. It reads: I love you. Night.

Suck in air. Hesitate. I can do this. Squinting through my tears, I dial her number. It rings. She picks up.

"Mom," I cry.

"What's wrong, baby?"

"I need you."

She sucks in a breath. "I'm leaving now. I can be there in three hours."

• • •

Mom wakes me the next morning.

Her light brown hair hangs loosely around her shoulders, and her lips are painted a pale pink. She's as beautiful as ever, but something's different. She's glowing. She's happy.

"French toast?" she asks, rubbing my shoulder.

I love the smells wafting into my room. Fresh coffee. Eggs. Bacon. "No, thanks," I reply. I don't deserve French toast.

"How about you take a shower, and then we'll get you some breakfast before your game," Mom says, threading my hair between her fingers.

"I'm not going," I reply, focusing on her beautiful face. It makes me feel better already. "How'd you know about the game?"

"Your brother told me you're managing, and I found the schedule on the refrigerator."

"I didn't even know he and Dad noticed."

She pushes hair off my forehead. "Why aren't you going to the game? I'd love to come with you."

Thinking of baseball makes me remember Brian and Drew and Will and Laura, and that makes the tears start up again. I cry so hard and for so long Mom has to get a towel from the bathroom because Kleenex isn't doing the trick. She doesn't press me, doesn't do anything but rub my back and kiss my head.

"Did you bring your dog? Annie?" I ask, sniffling.

"She stayed home with Theresa. She's a real sweet puppy—I hope you'll come meet her sometime soon."

"Mom? I'm sorry…for how I've acted. For not calling and all."

For judging you. For not thinking about your feelings.

Mom pats my knee. "No apology needed. I understand. I'm glad you called," she whispers. "I hate to think of you crying alone. What happened?"

I sniffle. Mucus clogs my throat. "When you hear what I did, you'll hate me."

"Impossible. Do you want to get out of the house and go for a walk before the game?"

"I'm quitting managing."

"You're no quitter."

"I already quit softball, you know."

"So you took a couple seasons off. Nothing wrong with that."

"You shouldn't be so forgiving. I'm an awful person." I let out a sob.

"You're one of the best people I know, Parker. You're compassionate and you love so hard."

"You don't know me anymore."

"People don't change that much. You're still the same loving Christian girl I've always known."

"How can you care about being a Christian after what happened with church? With what you did?"

"God still loves me," Mom replies quietly. "And He loves you too."

"Laura and Brother John said that—"

"Nothing they've ever said matters," Mom interrupts. "All that matters is your personal relationship with God."

"God hates me," I whisper, falling onto my pillow.

"I doubt that, but you need to work that out on your own. And no matter what, no matter what you've done, I'll never stop loving you, okay?"

I look up at her. "I love you too."

"I quit going to church," Mom admits quietly, averting her eyes.

"Why?"

"I can talk to God while I'm walking the dog or running in the woods just the same as if I'm at church."

I never thought of it that way. I guess it's true that I write to God all the time, He just doesn't listen. Or maybe He is, but He's telling me what I don't want to hear. I don't have to be at church to do that.

"What did Dad say when you showed up?" I ask.

"He said that you've been 'engaging in inappropriate activities with a guy named Corn Fritter.'" Mom laughs silently and shakes her head.

"Corndog. Will Whitfield."

"Isn't that the boy who drives you crazy? Always trying to beat you in school?"

"That's the one."

"Are you dating him now?"

"No." Fresh tears stream down my face. Mom pulls me into her arms and rocks me. "I wish I were though."

"Does he like you back?"

"He did…but I did something stupid. But you can't tell Dad or anyone," I mutter.

"I promise I won't say a thing."

Mom's face never changes as I tell her about Brian and Will and Drew, but I can tell she's upset because she squeezes my hand harder during the bad parts, like how I got myself involved with the coach of the baseball team.

"Did you sleep with him?" she whispers.

"No," I say, shaking my head.

"We should get you a doctor's appointment anyway. You're old enough that you need to go."

"Okay."

"We should probably get you on birth control too."

Holy embarrassment. "I won't be needing it."

"You should be prepared, just in case. I was seventeen once." Mom's mouth twitches in amusement, then goes back to sadness. "And you're sure Dr. Salter isn't planning a formal investigation?"

"He said he wouldn't if Brian resigned. It's all my fault." The tears won't stop. If I hadn't pursued Brian like I did…

"I'll call Dr. Salter here in a bit to make sure nothing will fall back on you. Brian is an adult and should've known better." Mom clutches my hand. "He shouldn't have taken advantage of you. This isn't all your fault, okay?"

"I messed everything up," I cry. "I lost Drew."

"So Drew is angry with you because of Will?"

"Right. But I'm mad at him too. He wouldn't even listen to me."

"I'm gonna tell you something that took me forty-two years to figure out." She traces the spiral pattern on my duvet. "Sometimes you gotta do what's right for you and forget about everybody else. All that matters is what you want. What you need."

What I had wanted was Brian, and look how that turned out. "That doesn't seem very Christian-like."

"Maybe. Maybe not. But you only live once, and if something feels right to you and you want it, you should go after it."

"Is that why you left us?" I cry. If she hadn't left, things would be okay. Maybe Will and I would've fallen in love.

"I never meant to hurt you," Mom replies, sounding so sad. "Sometimes I wish I hadn't done what I did, because losing you was the worst punishment possible." Her eyes close.

Mom did what she felt was right for her. Maybe it's about knowing what you want and going after it—and being willing to pay the consequences when everyone else thinks it's wrong.

"You didn't lose me," I say, hugging her as tightly as I can. And if God's watching us, maybe he's saying, *Sure, a bunch of shit had to happen, but a mother and daughter are back together.* A mother can love her daughter even if she's been sinning like it's going out of style. A daughter can love her mother even if she acted selfishly.

"I hurt Will so bad," I mumble, rubbing my face. It stings.

She pauses for a long moment. "Do you like him a lot?"

It felt like more than like. Something more, something real. Something like love. But now it's gone.

• • •

After I told Mom about Ryan's trip to the ER and what's been happening with him, her face went white, her eyes glossed over, and she stalked off to find Dad. They've spent a good hour talking in the dining room, using hushed voices. Ryan and I are sitting in the living room, trying to eavesdrop, pretending to watch TV, glancing at each other from time to time.

I miss Ryan. I wish he had noticed I disappeared with Brian, and had come to save me like that time I got lost at Opryland when I wanted to drive a Tin Lizzie. Ever since Mom left us, I've cooked his meals. I've done his laundry. He needed me to rescue him, while I kept waiting on him to save me again.

"You should've called me!" Mom says to Dad, and I see my brother cringe. He shuts his eyes. He never meant for this to happen, I know he didn't. Like me, he didn't know how to deal. He couldn't get the perfection back. So he changed for the worse. We both did.

I move from the love seat to the sofa where Ryan's sitting and wrap my arms around his neck and bury my face in his shoulder. He rubs my back and presses his face against my hair.

• • •

Nobody talks to me at school on Monday.

Everybody's too busy talking about me.

As if I don't feel guilty enough.

When I walk through the hall between classes, I hear my name. Brian's name.

"I heard she was sleeping with him," says a younger guy I don't know.

"Laura caught them doing it in the equipment shed!" says another.

"We lost our coach because of her," Paul says to Jake Sanders. "I can't believe we're stuck with the damned music teacher the rest of the season."

"She'll mess around with *anybody*," Matt Higgins tells Kristen Markum.

Dr. Salter calls me to his office after third period. He's playing with his paperweight again. "I've asked the faculty not to discuss Coach Hoffman's resignation with the students, but I've been hearing rumors all morning. Do you want to speak with the guidance counselor?"

"No, thank you," I tell him, bowing my head.

"I don't have any evidence anything actually happened…but I'm worried about you."

"I'm fine," I say quickly, quietly.

"I hope this dies down before graduation. I'd hate to have these rumors be the focus of graduation, rather than your valedictory speech and the other students' accomplishments."

When I peek up at his face, he swallows and looks out the window.

At lunchtime, I take a deep breath, and dragging my fingers across the white concrete walls, I head toward the cafeteria. I push the double doors open to find Will and Drew sitting together. I slowly walk to their table.

"I'm really sorry," I whisper.

Will scrunches his forehead, stands, and leaves the cafeteria without saying a word, abandoning his sandwich, chips, and apple.

I sit down across from Drew. He's still here. I hope that means he's willing to forgive me. Or at least let me explain that nothing was happening with Will.

"Drew," I say quietly. "I realize I've hurt you, but I need you to know I didn't hook up with Will. I swear I didn't."

He starts tearing up his paper napkin. "I'm just glad I didn't tell you that Corndog was interested in you."

I close my mouth to swallow. "You knew and you didn't tell me?"

"Does that mean you liked him back?"

"Don't my feelings matter as much as yours?" Just because he came out, I'm supposed to ignore everything I feel for Will? Is that what true friends do to each other? I touch my throat. "I wish I'd known he liked me."

"But you had Coach Hoffman. You would've just hurt Corndog. Like you'd hurt our other friends."

So this is what friendship is?

I thought friends gave you the benefit of the doubt. I thought friends stayed beside you through everything. I stayed beside Drew. At least I think I did. At least I tried. He's acting like Laura did.

"I'm sorry I hurt you and your friends," I say honestly. I stand up. "I'll see you around," I tell him.

I move to leave the cafeteria, wondering if Drew will blurt, "Wait." But he doesn't.

I chose not to act on a relationship with Will for him. I wish

Drew could've listened. I'm okay. It'll be okay. I'm panting. I lean up against the wall next to the gym, shutting my eyes.

That's when I decide to make Spring Break plans. To begin to try to heal from this mess, if healing's even possible.

• • •

Dad is way old-fashioned, so when I was growing up, he never wanted Mom to work a job. He wanted to make ends meet so she could stay home with Ryan and me, to drive us to tee-ball practice and to piano lessons, to help us with our homework after school. To cart us to teeth cleanings.

Up until this year, Ryan and I were pretty great, and we've always had excellent grades, so Dad did us right by asking her to be a home-maker. But I always knew Mom was itching for a job.

She loves gardening. Our front yard won the Franklin Beautification Award six years in a row, thanks to Mom's hedges and rose bushes. She wanted to learn topiary design but never got around to it because she was chauffeuring me to softball game after softball game.

I was so excited to find out that Mom recently got a job at a florist. It doesn't pay much, but she loves getting her hands dirty. The store's sales have skyrocketed since she started designing bouquets.

Mom and Theresa bought a place in Oldham, Tennessee, a tiny town smack dab in the middle of the Great Smoky Mountains. It's a close drive to Pigeon Forge, home of Dolly Parton and a buttload of outlet malls. It's also near Gatlinburg, where there's ice skating and great skiing. The cabin smells of cedar, and Mom made me a room here, with a cast iron twin bed and a shelf full of books.

She follows in behind me, carrying a short stack of towels. "Don't worry about anything. I'll cook and clean—all you have to do is relax."

"Thanks," I say with a nod. I give her a hug, and it feels better than being in any boy's arms. "Where's Theresa?"

"She went to visit her sister this week. I wanted some time to hang out with just you."

I bite back my smile. "I'm glad. Not that I don't like Theresa. Um—"

Mom waves a hand. "It's fine."

Annie the labradoodle follows me around as I check out the bathroom, kitchen, and dining room. I skip Mom's bedroom, because I'm not ready for that yet.

Mom steams some vegetables and grills chicken for dinner. We sit on the back porch overlooking the mountains to eat. Annie lies across my feet. I cut my chicken breast in half and pick at it, and Mom comments that I've lost a lot of weight.

I nod, avoiding her eyes, and eat a bigger piece of chicken. I decide to change the subject. "Did you always know?" I ask, popping a carrot in my mouth.

"Know what?" she asks.

"That you were different. That you didn't love Dad."

She chews and wipes her mouth. She stares straight ahead at the mountains. "I love your father. But yes, I think I've known for a long time. You need to understand that I was raised to believe I needed to marry a man, raise a family, and go to church."

"That's how I was raised."

Mom squeezes my hand. "And I'm telling you now that you should do whatever you want to do."

"That doesn't sound Christian. I want God to love me again."

"God does love you, sweetie. What I'm saying is, is if you want to be a Christian and have a relationship with God, you can do that. You have free will."

"Isn't there such a thing as too much free will? I shouldn't have gone after Brian. And look at Ryan."

"What happened with Brian is not your fault, understand? He's an adult." Mom's face goes hard. Sad. "And I don't want you to worry about your brother right now, okay? It's up to me and your father to help him. I know you care about him, but you're seventeen and have so many exciting things to look forward to. Graduation. Prom."

That's not technically true. I can't think of anything to look forward to. I lost Will. I lost Drew. Brian left me and didn't look back. I have no friends.

"How did you meet Dad, anyway?" I ask, spearing a piece of broccoli with my fork.

She smiles and sips her water. "I met him on the first day of college. We lived in the same dorm, on the same floor. He helped me carry my boxes up three flights of stairs."

"Then you got together?"

"Heavens, no. We were best friends for two years before he asked me out on a date, and he asked me to marry him senior year."

"But something felt off?"

Mom bows her head to think. "Your father and I should've stayed best friends instead of getting together. I still consider him my best friend now, even though I've hurt him so much I'm worried he'll never forgive me. I wish I had known back then that I had options. But my parents loved him. They still do. I thought marrying him would be enough for me."

I love the idea of having options and doing whatever I want, but do I have the courage?

The next morning while Mom takes a nap, when we should be at church, Annie and I run down a patchy dirt trail and through thick trees and alongside yellow daisies. I inhale the outdoors. Being out here in peace almost lets me forget about Will. I stop at a country market, where a little bell jingles against the glass door. I buy a bottle of diet lemonade, then walk back into the woods, sit down on a log, hug Annie's neck, and listen to a waterfall beating down on rocks.

"Pretty dog," I say, scratching her back. She pants and barks at a cardinal.

I pull the romance novel I brought out of my back pocket and settle in to read about lords and servants and corsets. This one duke guy is sleeping with the maid, but he can't marry her because she's the help, and aristocracy isn't allowed to have relations with the servant class, but no one knows she's really the Duchess of York or something. I hope she'll admit her heritage so they can get it on and have a legal marriage and all that jazz.

Annie rests her chin on my thigh, and I turn page after page, reading, but I can't stop thinking of Will. In these novels, all the problems could be solved if characters would talk to each other. I pull out my cell and send Will a text: I'm staying with my mom for Spring Break. Maybe we can talk when I get back? I miss you.

I sit on that log and finish the novel. The duke and the duchess end up together (obviously—the key to any good romance is a happy ending), but Will never texts back.

Dear God, I think, *Please…will you give my story a happy ending?*

I don't deserve a happy ending with Will after I used him to save Brian. To save me. But why hasn't he told Drew the truth? Have they talked about it?

I grab Annie's leash and trudge back to the cabin. Thinking of Will sucks, and it makes my eyes sting, but I'm okay. I like being outside with the dog. Maybe at college, I'll study to become a vet.

I'd work hard for that. Annie looks up at me and barks, and I'm glad that she likes me.

At Mom's cabin, before I put the romance novel back on the shelf, I study the cover, the duchess's sweeping blue gown. I want to wear Mom's white dress to prom, regardless if I have a date or not. My cell rings, and I pray it's Will calling to forgive me, or Brian calling to check on me, to find out if I'm okay. To tell me he's okay.

But it's Tate.

"I missed you today at church," he says.

"I'm spending some time with my mom."

We chitchat until he asks, "Have you talked to Drew lately? He stopped answering my texts and emails." Tate sounds so sad.

"I messed up bad," I say, and explain everything that happened with Brian, Will, and Drew.

"You didn't mess up bad. Sometimes things happen," he replies. "People make mistakes."

"I don't understand why Drew's acting like this. Why won't he talk to you?"

Tate says, "It's a hard thing—explaining to everyone who you really are. I've only told a couple of people." We stay silent for a bit before he speaks again. "Frankly, I think it's kinda hot you seduced an older man. Can I have one, please?"

I giggle, then go quiet. I stare down at the blue gown on the book cover and think about how much I want to wear my white dress. Maybe this is a chance for me to do what Mom said. Take care of myself. Do something for me.

"Hey, Tate?"

"Yeah?"

"Will you go to prom with me?"

• • •

Since Mom's still at the florist, I root around in the basement for more romance novels or a deck of cards, to play a game of Solitaire. It's Thursday of Spring Break, and nobody except for Dad and Tate has called. I'm so bored, I might borrow Mom's bike and try to find a movie theater. The nearest one is probably twenty miles away. I drag my finger over piles of board games and nonfiction books and baskets of linens. That's when I see it.

Mom's glove.

Her old softball mitt is sitting on a shelf next to a dusty vase. I hesitantly pick up the glove and slip my hand inside. I hunt around for a softball and find one behind a box of CDs. I pull a deep breath and start pounding the ball into the glove, loving the release, loving the energy whipping through my muscles. I rush up the stairs, taking two at a time, and jog out into the front yard. Giving Mom's tulip beds a wide berth, I throw the ball up into the air as high as it will go, then catch it. I do this over and over again. It never gets old.

Mom's car pulls into the driveway right when the sun begins to set.

"You didn't happen to bring your glove?" Mom asks as she steps out of the car.

"No."

She slides her tote bag onto her shoulder and comes to give me a hug and a kiss on the cheek. I've missed her doing that so much. "That's too bad. We could've played catch."

"Next time." I smile at her, but it's a pained smile. I wish I hadn't quit the team last year. I wish I hadn't let my former friends influence everything I did. I wish I had understood that people will always interpret my actions in different ways.

"There are public batting cages not too far from here," Mom says, pulling her glove off my hand. She slips her hand into it and pounds a fist against the pocket. "You pay for rounds of balls. It's fun—I go there sometimes."

"By yourself?"

"Yup." She beams. "Sometimes I even bat on the Major League Baseball setting. The balls come at you at 90 miles per hour."

My mouth falls open. "How many have you hit? Balls going at 90 miles per hour, I mean."

"A couple." She laughs softly and brushes her hair over her shoulder. "I usually out-bat the men who go there. It makes them all upset. And then they hit on me."

I grin. "Let's go."

"Let me change into sweats."

We hit ten rounds of balls apiece, blowing way too much money. I even try the MLB setting, but I only manage a foul-tip. I'm proud of it, though, considering how rusty I am.

Then Mom and I go out to this healthy buffet she likes, where we build giant salads full of tomatoes and squash and avocado to take home to eat in front of the TV. And for the first time in over a year, I watch a Braves game.

• • •

Dear Lord,

On Monday morning, when I get back to school, I'm going to talk to Coach Burns and Dr. Salter. I want to see if they'll give me another chance to play softball this year. I pray you'll be there with me when I ask. I know that being on a team means acting like a team player, which I haven't been this year. I'm the last

221

person who deserves to play softball. But I want to. I want to try.
And I hope I can help the team win some games.
Thanks for the great Spring Break.

Written on March 19 while overlooking the Great Smoky Mountains.
Burned using a candle.

the prom decisional

2 days until i turn 18

Dr. Salter and Coach Burns had the team take a vote.

Fourteen girls voted yes to letting me back on the team, while eight said no.

Now when I show up at softball practice, I don't pay one lick of attention to Laura. I bat, I run, I field the ball. I dive when I have to, jump when I have to, take risks when I have to. I cheer for my teammates during games. I chew my gum and smile and enjoy the bright sky.

Rumors about Brian and me haven't stopped, but I try my best to ignore them. I really try. But I cried myself to sleep one night after hearing Jake Sanders and Paul wondering aloud if Brian and I had ever had sex in the equipment shed. I cried again after I saw Will talking to Kate Kelly. I know he didn't see me, but I saw him, leaning against his locker, smiling down at her. I wish he would smile at me like that again.

I cried because, even though things were over between us before we got caught, Brian left without saying good-bye.

But I love this game, and I'm ashamed I ran away from it.

• • •

I didn't get a dinosaur invitation to Bo's party.

I didn't figure I would, but deep down I hoped. Still, I ride my bike over to Walmart, where I buy a package of baseball cards, some of those capsules that expand into animals in the bathtub, and a new Matchbox car. It's not much, and Will will probably think it's way over the top and that I'm trying to get his attention in *any* way, but that's not true. I like Bo, and I have a feeling that no one but my parents will notice my eighteenth birthday next week, and I don't want Bo to ever feel that way.

When you turn eighteen, you're supposed to go buy a lottery ticket. You're supposed to buy cigarettes, even if you don't smoke. Go clubbing with girlfriends in Nashville. Instead, I'll probably have a quiet dinner at home with Mom, Dad, and Ryan. And that's fine.

But as much as I want to take Mom's advice and do things for me and only me, I'm still lonely. I still need friends. When I go to college in the fall, I'll definitely be more social, but I will remain guarded. Was my connection with Brian real? Did we truly like each other? Does he miss me? I don't know if I'll ever get the *cojones* to reach out to anyone again, but if I care enough about the person to risk it, I'm open to the idea, and that's gotta count for something.

I pack the gifts in a bag and write *To Bo, from Parker Shelton* on it, then I ride my bike out to Whitfield Farms, loving the smell of cut grass floating on the warm spring air.

I pass a bunch of hay bales, then I stop at their mailbox, prop my bike up with one foot, and slip the gift bag inside. I stare at their house, remembering the Sunday lunch I had with them and the time Will had me over to baby-sit Bo. I softly touch the spot on my neck that he rubbed. My mind wanders to the time I nearly let him kiss me in the equipment shed, where everything fell apart, but I snuff

it out of my mind. I jerk my head from side to side, telling myself
to get over it.

I've tried. He's gone. That's it.

I take a final glance at the farm and say good-bye to Will Whitfield,
then I pedal home.

• • •

Friday's practice ends.

I hop on my bike and speed down the four-lane toward my
house. The sky is edging into twilight. When it's safe, I hold both
arms out like I'm flying. The warm wind rushes over my body, and
I'm smiling.

I pedal past Dairy Queen and get a major hankering for a Dilly
Bar. I do a U-turn and thrust my arms out again, pretending I'm a
bird. I've really lost it, but I don't care. It feels good.

I lock my bike and head inside, where I find Will and Drew
slumped in a booth, their trays piled high with food. They see me
and stare. Will stops chewing. Drew doesn't bite into the hot dog
he's holding. They look shocked. Probably because I've voluntarily
chosen a fast-food restaurant. My first instinct is to rush to my bike
and peel out of here, but I want that Dilly Bar. I haven't had one in a
couple years, and my taste buds are begging for the chocolate.

Heading to the counter, I avoid their faces. I don't even glance
back at them while I'm waiting for my order to come up. I smile to
myself, glad that even with all the weird stuff that happened between
Will and Drew, they're still hanging out together.

When the ice cream is in my hand, I peel back the paper wrapper
and bite into the chocolate shell. It cracks, and vanilla ice cream
flows onto my tongue. *Don't groan, don't groan,* I tell myself. But I
can't hold back my smile.

On my way out, I sneak a peek at Will and Drew. Drew's focused on his hot dog, but Will is watching me, one side of his mouth lifted into a subtle smile. He quickly averts his eyes and sinks his teeth into his burger.

That sucks, but I've got my ice cream and my bike and I'm heading home to my family. Maybe Dad will want to take a walk with me.

• • •

I stand on the third base line with my hand pressed over my heart. The national anthem is playing before the announcer reads the Prom Decisional lineup.

Coach Burns hasn't let me start very many games this season since I hadn't paid my dues and all, but he told me I'm definitely starting today.

Coach Burns never looks me in the eye.

The anthem ends, and the announcer says, "Thank you all for coming to the sixth annual Prom Decisional!" The crowd claps and whistles. The smell of popcorn wafts through the air. "It's also Senior Night here at Hundred Oaks. Coach Burns asks that parents of seniors join the players on the field."

Players who aren't seniors go sit in the dugouts, and this horribly cheesy instrumental music spills from the loudspeakers. Mom and Dad stand up from their seats in the bleachers and make their way onto the field. Brother John and Mrs. Martin move to stand next to Laura, ignoring my family. Ms. Bates joins Drew, while Mr. and Mrs. Whitfield, carrying Bo, smile and wave at me on their way to stand with Will. I guess they didn't hear the rumors about me.

Dad squeezes my neck, and Mom holds my hand. The announcer calls each senior's name, and Dr. Salter shakes our hands and gives each of us a little bouquet of roses. I invited Theresa to come, to stand next to Mom, but she graciously declined. And truth be told, that relieved me a bit. But I'm glad I asked her. I know Mom was glad too.

The bright lights shine down as we take the field. The boys are batting first. Sam steps up to home plate, taking a few practice swings. I bend over onto my knees, focusing on him, chewing my gum. Laura winds up and pitches a strong fastball right down the center. Sam watches it go by.

"Come on, Laura!" Jordan yells from the stands. "Strike him out!"

Sam smirks and takes another practice swing. JJ punches Jordan in the shoulder, and she shoves him. I stare Sam down. This time he swings and flies out to center field.

"Nice!" I say, smacking my glove. "Three up, three down, Laura."

The next batter up is Travis Lake. Laura takes a deep breath and gets ready to pitch. He hits a groundball to me, and I easily make the grab and hurl the ball to Allie at first. Two down.

Drew bats third, slamming a line drive over Mel's head. He stretches it into a double. Will bats cleanup but doesn't manage to clean anything up. He hits a line drive to Laura, and she catches it for out number three.

Coach has me leading off. Since I've shed a lot of weight, I've gotten way fast—fast enough to bat first. Jake Sanders pitches the softball overhand, which is kinda weird. I let the first pitch pass. On the second, I bunt and sprint down the first base line faster than Paul can pick up the ball and bomb it. Mom and Dad yell my name and clap. Mel is up next. She smacks the ball over the shortstop's head, and I hurl myself around second toward third. The left fielder launches the ball to Will at third. I slide into the bag right as Will tags my leg.

"Out!" the ump says.

I pull myself to my feet and brush the dirt off my pants. I give Will a quick smile before jogging to the dugout.

Our teams stay tied at zero-zero over the next three innings. In the fifth, Sam slams a homer over the left field wall. He showboats around the bases, dancing and acting up.

One-zero, Boys.

In the sixth inning, I hit a triple, knocking two runs in, and Allie also earns two RBI. In the same inning, Will hits a homer and brings Drew home. Before the eighth, the crowd sings "Take Me Out to the Ball Game." I'm having a great time, even if I'm not really speaking to anybody and nobody's speaking to me. As usual. It's just fine. I love this game.

In the top of the ninth, we're still up four-three with one out. Tim Keale hits a line drive straight into the hole. I lurch left and snatch the ball, then chase Will back toward second base. I outrun him, tagging his back.

"Out!" the ump yells.

We win!

My team rushes toward the pitcher's mound, screaming and hollering and jumping in circles. I smile to myself and pound the softball into my mitt.

"Good game," Will says, clapping my back and hustling toward the dugout. The guys I used to manage are packing up their equipment, acting like the game meant nothing. I can tell their pride is hurt. Will says something to the guys, and then they walk back onto the field. They start shaking hands with the girls and say, "Good game."

Sam asks Laura, "So what's the prom theme gonna be?"

"Disney," she replies, making everyone groan. And I mean everyone.

"Oh God," Will says, adjusting his cap.

"Wait," Allie says. "We need to discuss this as a team."

The girls huddle together, but I stay on the outskirts, not really caring. They're arguing, calling out all sorts of ridiculous themes. "Titanic!" "Christmas in May!" "Paris!" "Vegas!" "Cowboys and Aliens!"

Sam slips two fingers in his mouth and whistles. "Parker made the winning play. Let's hear what she wants."

"Ancient Rome," I say, grinning, thinking about the theme Sam has been jockeying for. "The decorations can be fake columns and gold lights and stuff."

"I like that idea," Allie says, and Mel nods.

"What about Disney?" Laura asks, bouncing on her toes.

"I dressed as Sleeping Beauty when I was, like, five," Sydney says. "It's been done."

"If we pick Ancient Rome, we'll all get to wear beautiful white gowns and crowns of ivy," I add.

"I love that!" Allie says.

"I can wear my gold strappy sandals," Mel replies.

"I have a white chiffon dress," Chelsea Clark says.

And the guys can show up in togas. I grin to myself.

"Sam," Allie says. "The theme is Ancient Rome."

He gapes and says in mock horror, "That's a terrible idea." Under his breath, he says to me, "Nice one."

Will lets out a laugh and gives me a quick smile, revealing the dimple I haven't seen in weeks.

I grab my bat bag and head toward my parents, running into Mr. and Mrs. Whitfield on the way. Bo's curled up in his mom's arms, playing with her necklace and sucking his thumb.

Mr. Whitfield shakes my hand. "I can't believe you made that double play. It was great."

"You need to come over for dinner sometime soon," his wife says. "It was so nice of you to give Bo a birthday present. Do you have something to say to Parker?" Mrs. Whitfield asks him.

He takes his thumb out of his mouth. "Thank you," he says, then deposits the thumb right back where it was.

"You're very welcome." It surprises me that the Whitfields are speaking to me, considering all the rumors flying around about what happened with Brian. I move to walk off but Mrs. Whitfield speaks again.

"We miss seeing you around," she says quietly. "Will hasn't said as much, but he's been down."

I give her a quick smile. "I miss him too," I mumble.

Trey is yanking on his mother's jeans and yelling something about a trip to McDonald's, so I excuse myself and go meet Dad and Mom. Her hug feels like the warmest blanket on the coldest night. *Thanks, God, for giving her back.*

going the distance

"I love it."

I pull the dress out of the box and hold it in front of my body. It's covered in blue and white flowers.

"It's a vintage ballerina dress. From the 1950s," Mom says, taking the full-bodied skirt between her fingers. "I figure you can wear it to graduation. We'll probably have to get it altered."

Dad looks pleased. He sips his coffee. I carefully place the dress back in its box.

"This is from me," Ryan says, pushing a gift bag across the table.

I dig through the pink tissue paper to find an envelope containing a gift certificate for a mani-pedi at Elizabeth Arden. "Thanks! It's perfect."

A smile flits across his face. I open Dad's present next. It's a new iPhone, something we can't even begin to afford.

I'm grinning like crazy. "Dad, this is too much."

"It's fine—your mom and I went in on it together." I jump out of my chair to give both of my parents a hug. Ryan lets me hug him too, and I'm happy that my family's together again. Maybe not in the way I wish we were together, but it's close enough.

"Cake and ice cream?" Mom asks.

"Sure," I reply, thinking I might eat the entire piece. I'm still not used to big portions, but I'll try. I blow out the candles, and the four of us dig into Mom's red velvet cake with cream cheese icing.

I hear a rap on the door. I swallow a bite of cake and go to answer it. I find Drew standing there. He hasn't knocked in years; he always lets himself right in.

"Hey," I say, stepping onto the porch. Moths flit around the porch light.

"Happy birthday," he says, passing me a gift wrapped in silvery paper. It makes me happy that he remembered.

"Is this from you?" I ask, hardly believing he got me a birthday present.

"Yes." He takes a step back and hops to the grass, avoiding my face.

"Should I open it now?"

"Whatever you want."

I stare at the gift. I glance up at him. "Thank you. I'd better get back inside." I point over my shoulder at the house.

"Okay. Good night." I step inside as he says, "Wait. I know the truth."

"The truth about what?" I reply, facing him again.

He slips his hands into his pockets. "That nothing had happened between you and Corndog. He told me the truth."

I nod slowly and bite on my lower lip, running my fingers over the silver wrapping paper.

"I just needed some time…to process everything, you know?" he says, glancing at my face.

I sit down Indian-style on the top stair of our stoop and slice open the envelope. Drew grabs a seat on the bottom step.

Before I read the card, I think about how Drew left me a couple weeks ago when I needed him most. How I've gotten stronger. He acted just like Laura did, and I'm not sure I want to have another friendship like hers, where the friend dictates everything. But Drew stayed with me when Mom went away. He only left me when his feelings were hurt terribly. I could've handled it better. Now he's back, and that sort of counts for everything.

The card reads, *It's not a real safari on the Serengeti, but it's the best I've got. Drew*

I take a breath. I slowly unwrap the silver paper to find a wooden kaleidoscope. I angle it toward the light and twist it, watching the red, purple, orange and blue spiral and mesh together. Animal shapes fill my field of vision. A giraffe, a hippo, and a turtle.

Maybe all friendships don't fizzle. Maybe, like the kaleidoscope, the colors just change.

• • •

In the library, I use the first part of lunch to Google Brian's name. Nothing new comes up, even if I restrict the search timeline down to the past month. Where is he? Did he find a job? Does he think of me? Does he hate me for the part I played in him losing his job? The part I played in the rumors? I think if I had one sign that Brian's doing okay, the guilt might dissipate a bit. But for now it's raging in my blood.

I look at the picture of him from when he played ball for Georgia Tech. Smile at his smile. Wherever he is, I hope he's happy.

I exit out of Google.

I go sit in the magazine room and start eating ham and Swiss on whole wheat, openly reading this awesome regency romance about gay dukes who have a thing for each other. I should loan it to Drew and Tate.

The idea brings a smile to my face. That's when Allie slowly approaches me, tangling her fingers together.

"What are you reading?" she asks.

I flash the paperback's front at her. I don't care who the hell sees. I love romance novels. She raises her eyebrows at the two shirtless buff men.

"Can I join you?" she says, gesturing at the chair across from me.

Months ago, I would've killed for her to ask that. But now? Eh. I care more about the two dukes than her. I do want friends. But I want friends who didn't abandon me when I needed them most.

"I'd rather read alone," I tell her. "Rain check?"

She chews on her lip. "Definitely. Yeah. See you." She trudges off, peeking over her shoulder at me, and I go back to my sandwich and book and drown myself in nineteenth-century London.

Best lunch date I've ever had.

• • •

Dad wakes me up on Sunday morning by pounding on my door.

"Come in," I blurt, burying my face in the pillow.

"It's church time."

I shake my head. "I'm not going."

"Okay, suit yourself." He kisses my forehead, then pauses. "I sent Veena an email asking if she'll come back to church."

I smile into the pillow, where Dad can't see. "I think that's a great idea. Wish I'd thought of it."

"Smart aleck," Dad says with a chuckle.

"Did she write back?"

"No."

I peek up and tell him I love him.

"I love you too," he replies, then disappears out the door.

I snuggle deeper under my covers. Dad respected my decision not to go. I can't believe it. I still have no idea why Dad continues to go to church. None. But he has a reason, and I should be okay with that, whatever it is. I hope Veena shows today—Dad's email is kind of a big deal. I bet it took a lot of courage to write to her like that. It kinda reminds me of the times Tate would call, to see why I wasn't at church. It's funny—I doubt his parents would care that much if he quit attending services and Sunday school. He must go for his own reasons. Maybe he likes hanging out on the playground and eating stale doughnuts. Maybe he likes organ music. Maybe he likes stained glass windows.

Maybe he likes praying silently.

Or hanging out with me.

"Wait!" I yell, hopping out of bed and yelling down the hall. "Dad, give me two minutes! I'm coming with you!"

Spending time with Tate, who became a real friend when I wasn't even watching, is a good reason to go. And I need to tell him about the pre-prom dinner reservations I made at Parthenon.

Plus, it'll make Dad happy, and that makes me smile.

• • •

The gym is decorated with fake Corinthian columns and lots of ivy and gold leaves and whatnot. Sam Henry's wearing a toga that sparkles à la Edward Cullen. His girlfriend, Jordan, is carrying a spear, and a bronzed shield is slung over her shoulder. Her blond hair is pulled up into a high ponytail. I can't believe she dressed up as a gladiator!

Bunches of dead Romans are probably rolling over in their graves.

"Man, our prom sucked compared to this," Tate says.

"You just wanted to wear a toga," I reply.

Tate grins. "Damn straight."

I smile down at him. "Punch?"

He takes my hand, and we make our way to the refreshments

table, not caring a lick about the people staring at us. He's four inches shorter than me, and he's wearing gold Converses to match his gold wreath and bracelets. Tate went all out.

He uses a ladle to pour me some frothy red punch, and then we go sit down at a table together. "Thanks for bringing me," he says, leaning close to my face. I notice him glancing around the gym.

"Are you looking for Drew?" I whisper.

He nods, sucking on his lip. "There's Will," Tate says, elbowing me.

He comes into the gym, wearing a ring of ivy on his head, straightening his crisp white toga. His arms are muscular and tan. He nearly trips over the long folds of cloth. I bring my fingers to my lips to cover my giggles.

"He didn't bring a date?" Tate asks. He puts a hand on my forearm.

"No idea." I sip my punch, hoping he didn't bring Kate Kelly. An ache fills my chest. From across the gym, his eyes meet mine. I remember Mom's words: *All that matters is what you want. What you need.* But I'm not sure that I deserve him. I hurt him bad.

Bottoms up. I gulp down my punch. "Will you excuse me?"

"Will you excuse me?" he asks, focusing on Drew, who's dancing with Amy.

"Yeah." I lift my skirts and edge around couples slow-dancing, keeping my breath steady as I head toward Will. I stop a few feet away and play nervously with my hair.

"Hey," I say.

He nods once and stares at the band. "Hey."

"Did you see Sam Henry? His toga is sparkly."

"Really?" Will gets up on tiptoes and scans the crowd. A look of revulsion crosses his face. "He never ceases to surprise me."

I rock on my feet. "It's amazing Jordan puts up with his silliness."

He lifts a shoulder. "She loves him."

Sam has his arms wrapped around her from behind. He's whispering in her ear and she looks so pissed, but it's a game they play all the time. Whatever he said makes her whip around and threaten him with her spear, then they're kissing softly and dancing. The way they're so natural together makes me envious.

I say, "Love makes you stupid sometimes, I guess."

"Sure does." Will's tone is harsh.

I give him a tiny smile. "I just wanted to say hi. Have a great prom, and I'll see you at graduation, 'kay?"

He raises his eyebrows. "Okay. Bye."

Pain rocks my chest. I leave him there and look for Tate. I find him talking with Drew. They're sitting at a table together, alone except for the flickering candles surrounding them. I fold my arms and smile, hoping they'll figure out if they like each other enough to risk being together. To risk facing all their friends and family and the church and the world. If he and Tate fall for each other, I'll be happy for Drew, and that's enough for me.

I pull my cell out of my purse and send Tate a quick text. Have fun. I'll be outside. Then I send Mom a text. Join me at prom?

She came to town this morning, to help me get ready. We spent the afternoon at a spa in Nashville. It was the most fun I've had in a long time. We both got French manis and pedis, and Mom said she thought I look beautiful. I think I do too.

Outside the gym, I sit on the steps and admire an oak tree, its leaves rustling in the warm wind. I prop my chin on my knees. Watch the fireflies. Listen to the crickets. I never imagined I'd come to senior prom to sit alone outside on hard concrete steps. I think about the whole world and wonder if anyone is out there for me. I shut my eyes and pray.

God, I don't want anything from you. I'm only saying thanks for giving me my mom back. Even though now I know she was never gone. And neither were you. I'm not happy that you had to test my faith this way, but you showed me what I needed most: Mom. Thanks for that.

A couple minutes later, she drives up and parks by the curb, then hops out of the car, sporting slim jeans and a white tank top. Her brown hair hangs long around her shoulders. She looks happy and beautiful. She sits down beside me and hooks her arm in mine.

"What's wrong?" she asks.

"Nothing's wrong. I just wanted to see you." I clutch her arm and check out the stars.

She rests her head against mine. "Where's Tate?"

"Talking to Drew. I didn't want to interrupt."

"And there's no one else you want to hang out with in there?"

"Not really. Well, maybe Will, but I need to move on…It sucks that everything probably would've worked out with him, you know, if I'd acted normal after you left."

"I wish I'd gotten to know him before this happened," Mom murmurs.

My stomach grumbles.

"Ice cream?" she asks with a smile.

"We should buy a banana split to share."

Mom stands and puts out a hand. I get to my feet and wipe the dirt off my dress, then lift my head to find Will standing here watching me.

I rush to ask, "How long have you been standing there?"

He cracks his knuckles. "A while."

I smooth my dress, and Mom slips an arm around my waist, but doesn't move to introduce herself or speak.

But Will, ever the gentleman, extends a hand to her. "Ma'am, you might not remember me. I'm Will Whitfield."

Mom shakes his hand, not smiling. "I'm Christy."

"We're getting ice cream," I tell him. "I'll see you arou—"

"Wait!" he blurts. "I wanted to see if you'll dance with me…?"

"I couldn't do that to your date. It's not right."

"I didn't bring a date."

Mom pats my back and goes to lean against her car. Leaving me alone. With him.

"You brought a date, huh?" he asks, jerking his head toward the gym.

"I brought him more for Drew's sake than mine."

Will moves a step closer. His blue eyes focus on mine. "You're a good friend."

"Or at least, I tried to be a good friend." I choke the words out.

"I know you did," he says softly.

"I'm sorry I wasn't a better friend to you. I was messed up. The whole situation was messed up."

"Yeah…" He steps so close I can smell the Downy Mrs. Whitfield must've used when she washed his toga.

"But you gotta know," I say, "I started falling for you that night you walked me home from that party."

"Really? Why didn't you tell me?"

I whisper, "Because that night Drew told me he liked you."

Will drops his head.

I say, "I couldn't do that to him. Not after what he'd just told me. He's my best friend." I'm shaking my head and covering my mouth now. Wishing Mom would come take me by the arm and force feed me ice cream.

"I get why you needed to wait to talk to Drew," Will says. "About me, I mean."

"I understand that you were hurt about Brian and me, but I wish you could've trusted me and let me have the time to figure that stuff out. I was going to say yes to prom. I wanted to go with you so bad."

His expression fades to soft. There's a long pause before he says, "About that dance?" He rubs his palms together.

I glance over my shoulder at Mom. "Just a sec," I tell him. Gathering my skirts up in my hands, I zip over to her. "He wants to dance. Can we get ice cream tomorrow instead?"

She fluffs my hair. "I'll be waiting up. I'll want all the details, understand?" She gives me a mischievous smile and a hug.

"Definitely," I whisper into her shoulder.

I break away from her to find Will crossing his arms over his stomach and a rush of shame washes through me because I hurt him so much. But all I can do is try to be the best me I can be.

"I'd love to dance," I say.

We don't touch each other until we reach center court in the gym, where it feels like hundreds of eyes are focused on us. But I shut them out. This is my dance, and they can't stop me from enjoying it. A Kenny Chesney song is playing as I stretch my arms around his neck. He sets his hands on my hips, and like in eighth grade, his hands are trembling. We sway back and forth, finding a beat (which is hard 'cause his toga is basically a dress and his legs keep getting tangled). I inch closer and closer to him, to rest my head against his partially-covered chest. His hands shake. I pull my arms from around his neck, and he scrunches his eyebrows at me before I place my hands over his, on my waist, to still them. Our eyes meet. I run my fingers up his arms to his neck.

I catch Drew and Tate checking us out. Drew waves at me, a meek, sincere smile on his face, and goes back to chatting with Tate.

"Hey," I whisper to Will.

"Hey." A smile edges on his mouth.

"Can we go outside? I don't want Drew to have to watch us dancing together."

He takes my hand and leads me out back into the school parking lot, behind the gym. "You're a sweet girl. And a good friend." Under the street lamps, beside the Dumpsters, he pulls me into a clumsy waltz, the best he can do in his silly toga. He gets a grossed out look on his face.

"What are you thinking about?" I ask.

He glances around at the pavement. "I was wondering where exactly Henry found that hot pink dildo."

I slap his chest, making him laugh, and we move closer and closer.

When we stop, I say, "I kinda lied."

He loosens his grip on me, and begins to pull away, looking hurt, so I get up on tiptoes and lightly peck his lips. Because I want to. Tingles rush over my skin, and he moans from deep in his throat. We break apart and smile at each other.

"More?" Will whispers, then gives me another quick kiss. My hands are in his hair, and his eyes are hazy with happiness. "What did you lie about?"

I adjust his crown of ivy. "I wasn't just falling for you…I think I loved you."

He digs fingers into my waist and yanks me closer, acting all sexy alpha male.

"I was getting there," he replies with a husky voice, sweeping his hands over my back. "Love, I mean."

"You think you could get back to that place?"

He nods, brushing his lips against mine. "Could you get back?"

I can do whatever I want.

acknowledgments

Thank you, as always, to Sara Megibow and everyone at Nelson Literary Agency for their support, enthusiasm, and advice. Much gratitude to my editor, Leah Hultenschmidt. I'll never forget the look on your face when I told you what this book is about. Your eyes popped open wide and you looked so excited! I am so grateful to Trish Doller—I'm glad you love Corndog, and thanks for your help in making this book strong. Many thanks to Allison Bridgewater, Sarah Cloots, Rekha Radhakrishnan, Maria Cari Soto, Andrea Coulter, Tiffany Schmidt, Christy Maier, Holly Longstreth, Rebecca Sutton, Madeleine Rex, Erica Haglund, Kari Olson, Jessica Wallace, Robin Talley, and Jessica Spotswood for reading my work and offering great advice. Dad, thanks for loving this book, even though it's something you normally would never, ever read in a bazillion years. Thank you to Sourcebooks for giving my books a great home.

Thank you to my husband, Don, for reading every word I write and always supporting me. I could not do this without you.

And finally, many, many thanks to my readers! I am humbled by the feedback and support you have given me. You rock.

about the author

Miranda Kenneally grew up in Manchester, Tennessee, a quaint little town where nothing cool ever happened until after she left. Now Manchester is the home of Bonnaroo. Growing up, Miranda wanted to become an author, a Major League Baseball player, a country music singer, or an interpreter for the United Nations. Instead she became an author who works for the US Department of State in Washington, DC, and once acted as George W. Bush's armrest during a meeting. She has a degree in International Relations from American University. She enjoys reading and writing young adult literature and loves *Star Trek*, music, sports, Mexican food, Twitter, coffee, and her husband. Visit www.mirandakenneally.com.